AFTER THE DANCE

Donna Deloney

Proverbial Press

CHICAGO, ILLINOIS

Donna Deloney/Proverbial Press
www.DonnaDeloney.com

Publisher's Note: This is a work of fiction. Names, characters, places, and incidents are a product of the author's imagination. Locales and public names are sometimes used for atmospheric purposes. Any resemblance to actual people, living or dead, or to businesses, companies, events, institutions, or locales is completely coincidental.

After the Dance/ Donna Deloney. -- 1st ed.
ISBN 979-8-9887125-0-3

Mama Dear, thank you for always believing in me.
Love,
your Baby

For Aunt Ruby, who let me sneak her Harlequin novels
when I was a kid;
and Aunt Dee, who fed my reading habit and introduced me to
lots of amazing books.

I'll be forever grateful.

ONE

"Geez, how many times do we have to go through this? You should know it already!"

Stacy's head snapped up from her phone. She signaled for the music to stop. "What's the problem, Arianna?"

The teen's face scrunched into a scowl. "It's these *babies*! Kenzie missed a turn and she threw the whole line off."

"I'm sorry," Kenzie said. The eight-year-old swiped at the tears on her plump cheeks.

Stacy signed. The junior and senior dance teams had been working on their finale for the gala for weeks. For juniors like Arianna, there was a lot riding on the success of tonight's performance. For the younger dancers like Kenzie, this was their first performance before an audience and their nerves were showing.

"Let's run the last sequence again." Stacy hopped on the stage. With her back to her students, she counted down, then quickly executed the last eight counts of the dance. "Back in position, everyone." She waited until the kids repositioned themselves before hopping down. "Five, six, five, six, seven, eight." The music played and the dance teams performed the steps exactly as they'd been taught.

"Beautiful." She glanced at her watch. "Let's take a break. Those of you who have homework—and I know most of you do—get to it. The rest of you stay quiet so you're not disturbing those who are working. Mrs. Green and Mrs. Baldwin are available if you need help. There are also snacks, but don't overload. Dinner will be served right after your performance. Understood?"

"Heard," the children responded.

"Excellent," she said. The children began filing off the stage. "Arianna, a word."

The teen who had spoken up came downstage, hopped down and stood in front of her. "You were out of line, Arianna." Before the girl could speak, Stacy held up her hand. "You weren't wrong that Kenzie should know the sequence, but you were wrong in how you handled it." She placed a gentle hand on her student's shoulder. "I know how important tonight is to you. You've worked hard and you'll get your shot. But if you're planning to make dance your career, you cannot do it at the expense of your fellow dancers. The best dancers in the world are not the ones with the most talent. They're the ones who try to make other dancers around them be great." She lifted the girl's chin so she could see directly into her eyes. "You are a leader. I expect you to act like it. Understood?"

"Heard. I'm sorry," Arianna replied, chastened.

Stacy smiled. "I know you are. That's why you're a leader. Now go take a break and make it right with Kenzie. She needs a dose of your confidence." She gave the girl a quick hug then walked away, glancing again at her phone. More texts. *I'll be so glad when this is over.* Between corralling the student performers and their parents, making sure her special guest performer had all her needs met, and seeing that her VIPs—creative directors, scouts, and department chairs of several dance and music conservatories—had prime seats for the gala, it was making her head hurt.

"It's going to be fine," Toye Hawkins said, handing Stacy a bottle of water. "It always is."

Stacy took a swig. "How is it you always know what I'm thinking?"

"Because I've been your best friend since seventh grade. And because you go through this every year. You're so busy you forget to stay hydrated. I'm also betting you haven't eaten anything since this morning."

The thought of her long-ago eaten cinnamon and chocolate muffin and French vanilla latte made her stomach growl. "Guilty as charged, counselor." She looked over at the table where the silent auction was being held. "How are we looking? Did we get some interesting items for bid?"

Toye nodded. "Thanks to my brilliant networking skills, we managed to get some box seats for the Crosstown Classic between the Cubs and Sox. We've got sideline passes for a Bears pre-season game, along with dinner cruise tickets, Broadway in Chicago memberships, a weekend hotel stay and other delightful items for our heavy hitters. And we've got some other fun experiences, including a free dance lesson from you."

"That should bring in about ten dollars," Stacy said, chuckling.

"You underestimate yourself. If they knew they were getting a lesson from the great Anastasia—"

"But they aren't," Stacy said, her tone harsh. "It's one lesson with Stacy Roberts, the creative director of CCA. That's it. I need to check on Mom." She brushed past her friend in a rush, blinking back tears along the way.

TWO

"Dude," Eric Woodson said, "Can you please pick up the pace? I'd like to get there before the program starts."

Cooper Banks came out of his bedroom holding up two ties, one with a silver and black paisley pattern, the other was black and red striped. "I thought you said it didn't start until seven. Which one?"

Eric sighed. "The program starts at seven, but the cocktail hour and silent auction start at six. It's way out in the south suburbs and with traffic, we should get moving." He looked at his friend's tie choices. "Go with the silver."

"You don't think it's too much?"

Exasperated, Eric threw up his hands. "Then go with the black! I don't care! Man, with all your loot, you'd think you could afford to hire somebody to pick your clothes out for you. You've been this way ever since I've known you."

"First impressions," Cooper said, flashing a grin.

"Whatever." Eric chuckled as Cooper retreated to his bedroom. He'd been best friends with Cooper since their freshmen year at Morehouse College. All through high school, Cooper kept his head in the books and his eyes on the stock market, making his first million before his eighteenth birthday. Going into college, he had never really mastered the social graces, especially those for an up-and-coming financial wizard who just happened to be an African American. Eric had taken him under his wing, helping his new friend develop street sense and his own fashion style. Cooper had always been more comfortable in Levi's than Armani, but as his confidence and financial status grew, Eric convinced Cooper to update his wardrobe so he would at least look the part of a soon-to-be-billionaire. But in new social situations, Cooper sometimes reverted to the geeky eighteen-year-old with no confidence in his choices.

Even with all his money, Cooper remained the most down-to-earth person Eric had ever met. Cooper never flaunted his wealth and wasn't seen flashing his money around. Other than a Mercedes Benz SUV and sedan, his one indulgence was owning season tickets courtside at most of the NBA arenas. Occasionally, he'd fly in and catch a game. Most of the time, he donated the use of the seats to a worthy cause. "By the way," Eric said, "did I thank you for donating the courtside seats to the Bulls/Bucks game to the silent auction?"

"You did," Cooper replied, emerging from his bedroom. He'd opted for a completely different tie. "Why do I have to go? You know I prefer to keep these things anonymous."

"No one will know it's from you. My friend assured me that your name will not be associated with the donation."

"Then why do I have to go?"

"Because I must go to represent the hospital since they're a sponsor. My date had a work emergency, and I don't want to go alone. And don't you want to know more about the…" he pulled out his tickets, "Chi City Arts? That's who you donated the tickets to." He ignored his friend's groan. "Look, there's a bar, food, live jazz, and Twila Dee will be there. If she looks as good as she sounds, mercy." He fanned himself and Cooper punched him in the shoulder.

"That girl is young enough to be your daughter, you hound."

"True, but she is legal. I'm kidding! Listen, for real, Chi City Arts is making a name for itself as a school for developing new talent in the arts. I read that Twila was one of its first students and look at her now. You saw the news story about that young guy from Englewood who started playing violin at CCA. He's making his debut with the Chicago Philharmonic this season. You know how rare it is to see a young black man playing in an orchestra, much less a world-famous one? That's dope, man."

Cooper held up his hands. "Okay, you sold me. Let's get going before I change my mind."

"Cool. Listen, if you don't have a good time, I'll make it up to you."

"How?"

"I'll let you take me to the next Bulls/Warriors game. I'll buy the beers."

THREE

Stacy's visit to the lobby outside of the ballroom filled her with a measure of peace. Despite all the chaos inside the ballroom, the outside was humming along with energy and efficiency, thanks to Rose Robinson's organized efforts. Now, she was overseeing the display on the table. "That side of the tablecloth is uneven," she pointed out to one of the staff members. She called out to a parent, "Gail, please make sure that every seat inside has one of the new brochures." She reached down and handed the woman a box. "Here are extras. Make sure there are some at the silent auction table." As the woman took off, Rose looked over and saw her daughter. "Whew, chile. It's more than a notion to pull this off every year."

Stacy gave her mother a side hug. "We couldn't do it without you, Ma." She gave the older woman a kiss on the cheek. "You need anything?"

Rose shook her head. "We've got it under control. We're just about done." She took a quick glance at her daughter. "What about you? How are you holding up?"

Stacy nodded. "We're good for the most part," she said, deflecting from her mother's knowing gaze. "The kids are done rehearsing and they're backstage. Toye's got the silent auction covered. I'm just waiting for our musical guest to arrive so she can do her soundcheck."

"We're here," a young woman's voice called out. Stacy grinned as three-time Grammy winner Twila Dee made her way over. She hugged Stacy. "I'm so sorry. We were in the studio and lost track of time."

"You're fine, T, but the cocktail hour is in about twenty minutes. I hope that's enough time."

"It's fine," Twila said. "Hey, Mama Rose."

"Hey, Twila," Rose said, giving the young woman a hug.

"Ooh, nobody gives hugs like Mama Rose." Twila gestured to her band. "Why don't you guys go in and get set up. I'll be in shortly."

"I can't thank you enough for being here, T," Stacy said.

"Are you kidding me?" Twila replied. "You know I couldn't turn down you and Mama Rose. I'll always be grateful for you and CCA. Without you, I don't know where I would've ended up. Definitely not where I am now." She brushed back a tear and Rose quickly enveloped her in another hug.

"Hush," Rose said. "God knew the path he set you on. You were always destined for greatness. We just helped you to get there."

"Stop or you'll have me boo-hooing all over the place," Twila said, pulling back, twisting her signature rainbow braids down her back.

Stacy laughed. "You're still such a crybaby," she teased. "You better get going. I'll check with you backstage. There are some excited kids ready to meet you."

"I'm looking forward to it," Twila said before heading into the ballroom. As she left, Rose said to Stacy, "You did that."

"God did, Mama." She checked her watch. "Shoot, I need to make sure the string ensemble gets set up for the cocktail hour."

"I'll go," Rose said. "I need to go the bathroom anyway before the madness starts. Can you keep an eye on things?"

"I've got it, Mama." She took a seat and glanced around. Everything was in order. Mama Rose made sure that everyone knew what to do and how to do it. Staff, parents, and volunteers worked seamlessly to make sure the gala was a success, not just for CCA, but because no one wanted to let Stacy or Mama Rose down.

FOUR

As they rounded the corner towards the ballroom entrance, Cooper pointed out all the people still setting up in the lobby. "I told you we were too early. They're still setting up."

Eric shrugged. "You know how I feel about that. To be early is to be on time."

"And to be on time is to be late. I can't believe you're still quoting *Drumline*."

"Says the man that know *The Godfather* by heart," Eric replied.

"Hey, *The Godfather* is a classic." Cooper launched into his best impersonation of the late Marlon Brando. Rubbing the underside of his chin, he said, "'I'm gonna make him an offer he can't refuse.'" He started laughing and Eric shook his head.

"It's a good thing you're rich," Eric said. "Your impressions are horrible."

They approached the table where Stacy was busy pinning up Kenzie's hair. She spun the young girl around to face her. "There you go, sweetie. You're all set. You're going to do great." She gave the girl a quick hug. "Now get back inside before Mama Rose sees you out here by yourself."

"Okay, thank you," Kenzie replied. She skipped off and Stacy turned her attention to the men standing in front of her. "Good evening, gentlemen. How can I help you?"

"I'm Dr. Eric Woodson from Lurie Children's Hospital. This is my friend, Cooper Banks."

Stacy smiled at them and grabbed a clipboard. Scanning a list, she saw Eric was listed as a VIP with a plus-one by his name. "Dr. Woodson, Mr. Banks, welcome. We're not quite ready, but if you'd like to go to the bar and have a drink, you're more than welcome. You can also start bidding in our silent auction." She handed them each a program.

Eric took his, but Cooper remained stock still. He gazed at Stacy, taking in her smooth ebony skin and dark brown eyes that seemed to take in everything. He noticed a dimple that hung like a crescent moon in her left cheek and how her messy auburn curls framed her round face. Though she wore no makeup, save for a neutral lip gloss, she was stunning. He didn't realize he was concentrating so hard until he felt Eric nudge him.

"Coop, you alright, man?" Eric whispered.

Cooper blinked and nodded. "Yeah," he muttered. He saw her still standing with the outstretched program. "Uh... thanks."

Eric rolled his eyes. "Come on." He dragged his friend towards the bar.

"Who was that?"

"Probably one of the parent volunteers," Eric said, shrugging. He smirked at his friend. "She lit a fire in you, huh?"

"She is beautiful," Cooper admitted.

"Why don't you go talk to her?"

"She's probably busy with her kids. Let's get that drink."

❧ ❧

Mama Rose took the clipboard from Stacy. "And who were those handsome gentlemen," she asked, winking at her daughter.

"Don't go there, Mom. The guy in the gray suit is Dr. Eric Woodson. He's one of the VIPs from the children's hospital."

"And the other one?"

"His date, I guess."

Rose shook her head. "What a waste."

"Mom!"

"I'm just saying. Those fine-looking men look like they'd make beautiful babies."

"Mother please!" Stacy shook her head. "I need to get ready. Please make sure they get their VIP swag bags."

FIVE

Stacy was glad she built an hour into the schedule to get ready for the gala. It took thirty minutes to straighten out her unruly curls. Then she styled her hair into a messy bun. Checking her watch, she quickly added her makeup then slipped into her dress. She loved the way the black cocktail dress fit her frame. The sequins on the bodice shimmered in the light, while the handkerchief skirt swished around her toned legs. A wistful smile crossed her face as she remembered how she looked and felt in a similar dress. Only instead of the strappy heels she was currently wearing, she was in toe shoes, gliding across the stage.

Shaking her head, she gave herself another quick once-over in the mirror. Satisfied with her appearance, she sailed out of the dressing room with ten minutes left in the cocktail hour. She greeted familiar faces, parents and supporters, members of CCA's board of directors, sponsors and family and friends of the performers. She made her way over to Toye, who was working her magic at the silent auction. She marveled as her best friend, one of the city's fiercest defense attorneys, convince a man to bid on several different items in the auction. After he left, she sidled up to Toye. "You could sell bacon to a vegetarian."

Toye laughed, flinging her braids behind her. "It wasn't that he didn't want to bid. He had to be convinced on *how much* he wanted to bid on the items he wanted most. Once I reminded him his donation would be supporting at-risk youth *and* he'd get at great tax write off, he didn't hesitate to bid big." She lowered her voice. "We're gonna rack up tonight."

"We always do with you heading the auction," Stacy said.

"Yeah, but tonight, I have a feeling we're going to really clean up." She pointed where Eric and Cooper were standing near the bar. "Do you know who that is?"

Stacy nodded. "Sure. That's Dr. Eric Woodson from Lurie Children's Hospital. He's representing one of our sponsors."

"Not him. The other guy in the killer black suit."

"I think it's his boyfriend."

Toye's eyes grew large. "Are you kidding me? Cooper Banks isn't gay." Her brow furrowed. "At least I don't think he is." She pulled out her phone and quickly tapped in some information. She held it out for Stacy to see. There were dozens of photos of Cooper Banks at some event or another, each with a different beautiful woman at his side.

"Okay, so he's been seen with lots of women. It's not the first time someone has used a woman to hide the fact that he's gay."

"Girl, stop. I don't care what he is, I care *who* he is, and so should you." Toye took her phone and tapped once more. "I can't believe you don't know who he is." She handed the phone back to Stacy.

Stacy scrolled through the headlines. Cooper Banks had done well for himself. Very well. He had made several Forbes lists over the years, including "30 Under 30," "Forbes 400," and "The Midas List." According to one article, he was slated to land on the next "Billionaires List." She handed the phone back to her friend. "He's rich. Why would you think he's going to bid on the auction? What do we have that he doesn't already have or have done?"

"He's here for a reason, Stacy. In fact," Toye checked her list, "I'd even bet money that he donated these courtside seats to a couple of Bulls' games. I've read that he holds courtside seats at several arenas including Madison Square Garden. When he's not using them, he donates them to worthy causes to use as gifts or prizes."

"Why did he donate to us? I doubt if he's ever heard of CCA before showing up here tonight."

"Maybe his friend convinced him to do it. Doesn't matter. If he's here, I think we can count on a sizeable donation."

"I'm not counting on it." Stacy checked her watch. "I need to wrap up the classical ensemble and get the program started. Keep up the excellent work."

"I'll do what I can. You need to go over there and make nice with that man, boyfriend or no," Toye said.

Stacy rolled her eyes. "Yes ma'am." She drifted over to where Eric and Cooper were standing. "Dr. Woodson, Mr. Banks, welcome. Are you enjoying yourselves?"

Eric smiled. "Yes, we are. Didn't we just meet outside?"

"Not formally." She extended her hand. "I'm Stacy Roberts, the CEO and Creative Director for CCA."

"It's a pleasure to meet you, formally," Eric said. "You already know my awkward friend, Cooper Banks."

"It's nice to meet you, Mr. Banks. And let me take this opportunity to thank you for your kind donation to our auction," Stacy said, shaking his hand. An unfamiliar warmth spread through her like never before.

"It was my pleasure, Ms. Robinson," Cooper said, cutting his eyes at Eric. "I had hoped to keep it anonymous."

"It wasn't Dr. Woodson. It was my friend, Toye." She pointed at her friend, who looked up and gave a small wave.

"She figured out who you were and that you had made the donation. It was very generous of you."

"I'm happy to support such a worthy cause," Cooper said, enjoying the softness and strength of her hand in his. "I'd like to discuss other ways to support you...and CCA," he added quickly.

Stacy's grin remained in place, even as she extricated her hand from his. "I'm sure we can work things out. If you'll excuse me, I need to get the show on the road." She left him standing there, his gaze following her every move.

❧ ❧

Eric tapped his friend on the shoulder. "What is it with you and that woman? Every time you get around her, you revert to being a teenager."

Cooper shook his head. "There's something about her. I can't explain it. I've never felt anything like it."

"I get it. She's hot."

Cooper shook his head. "Beautiful, yes. Stunning, yes. But it's more than that."

"Right. CCA is her baby. You've been looking to diversify your portfolio. Why not offer up some financial support?"

"I'll be glad to help," Cooper said, "but I want to get to know her."

"You're the man, Coop," Eric replied. "If you're feeling some kind of way about her, do something. Be Cooper Banks. Find a way to get her attention." He glanced over to where Toye was overseeing the auction. "I have an idea."

SIX

Stacy stepped up on stage and positioned herself at the microphone. "Welcome to the Chi City Arts annual gala," she began. She paused for the thunderous applause before continuing. "We are so excited to have each of you here with us, whether it's your first time or tenth. As one of Chicago's premier non-profit arts organizations, we are so proud of the work of our teachers and our staff, but more importantly, our students. They are the reason we are here tonight. They have put in the work in their respective crafts to share with you and I can't wait for you to see the fruits of their labor.

"For some of our students, CCA is an opportunity to get out of the streets and explore their creativity. For others, it's a chance to develop their talents and create scholarship opportunities. And for a few, it's the gateway to a career in the arts. It's especially true of our special guest, Grammy-award winner Twila Dee."

Grinning, she let the applause die down before speaking again. "Twila had the God-given gift of singing, but she was painfully shy. CCA helped give her the self-confidence she needed to perform through our recitals and events such as our gala. Many of you were here when she made her debut performance. Tonight, she returns as a CCA alum and accomplished artist with a skyrocketing career with many more years to come. As you'll see from some of our performances, we may be witnessing the next Twila Dee, or the next Misty Copeland, or the next Questlove. And even if that's not the case, the arts and what we're teaching at CCA will carry over for a lifetime.

"Alright, I've talked enough. You'll be hearing more from parents, board members, and students throughout the evening. Thank you again for sharing your evening with us. We have lots of surprises and fun in store for you this evening. Now, let's get on with our program!"

As she took her seat, she glanced out in the audience, only to find Cooper staring at her. A sudden heat flushed in her face, causing her to grab her goblet of water and guzzle it down. Even with her back to him, she could still feel the intensity of his gaze. What did he want from her? She couldn't be sure, but she knew she needed to avoid him at all costs.

☙ ❧

Eric elbowed Cooper. "Would you stop staring at her," he whispered. "You're giving me the creeps. I can't imagine how she feels."

Cooper blinked. "What? What did you say?"

"I said, stop staring at that woman. Pay attention to what's happening on the stage."

"I don't know what it is about her," Cooper said.

"You've seen beautiful women before," Eric replied. "You've even dated a few of them."

That much was true. Cooper, despite his reticent nature, had dated many beautiful women, as attested in the media and tabloids. Some of his past relationships had lasted months. But he hadn't desired to commit to anyone long-term, and after a while, he realized that most of his dates were more interested in his money and status rather than getting to know him. He hadn't minded the attention, but he'd grown weary of being someone's path to Insta-fame. Lately, Cooper had been flying solo, ducking questions about his relationship status. The thought of being seen with Stacy on his arm sent a warmth through him he hadn't felt in… forever.

Stacy was back on stage again. This time they were announcing the winners of the silent auction. Cooper desperately hoped Eric's plan worked.

ꕥ

Toye handed Stacy the last envelope from the auction. Toye whispered, "I told you we were going to clean up. Check out the winning bid for you."

Stacy glanced down and resisted the urge to gasp. The winning bid for a private dance lesson with her was more than most of the other auction bids combined. Mindful of the fact that everyone was waiting, she plastered a smile on her face. "I know you've all been dying to know the winner of the private dance lessons from yours truly." She could hear the laughter and applause, so she plowed on. "The winning bidder is Mr. Cooper Banks!"

She clapped along with the audience as Cooper made his way onto the stage. As he shook her hand, a jolt of electricity coursed through her, causing her stomach to flip flop. He held her hand for a moment longer than he needed to, then smiled and released her without saying a word before heading back to his seat. "Thank you all for your bids. Please know that your contributions will be used to provide scholarships for our students and will go a long way to help us build our new facility. We've had a great meal and wonderful performances from our students, haven't we?" The audience cheered loudly for the kids, some even standing to their feet. She waited until it died down, before saying, "I know you're as excited as I am to welcome to the stage, our very special guest, CCA's very own Twila Dee!" She greeted the young artist, then headed for her seat.

As Twila and her band began the intro to her first number, Stacy pulled out the paper that Toye had given her with the bids. She swallowed hard at the number. Cooper Banks had put in a bid for $25,000 for a private dance lesson with her. The second highest bid was $75. As she tried to focus on Twila's number, she had a thought: *What are you up to, Cooper Banks?*

SEVEN

As the gala wrapped up, Stacy took time to greet the students and commend them on a job well done. Many of the teens were basking in the praises of CCA's sponsors and the representatives from the various programs that had been invited. Stacy noticed Arianna and her parents speaking to several of the college and dance academy reps.

Stacy grinned when Kenzie ran up to her. She embraced the young girl and said, "You were wonderful, Kenzie."

"I didn't forget the steps," she replied breathlessly. "Arianna helped me, and I got it right!"

"You most certainly did. I'm very proud of you."

Her parents came up behind her. Her mother had tears in her eyes. "I want to thank you, Ms. Robinson. You don't know how much this means to our daughter. She loves to dance, but we couldn't afford most of the ballet schools we investigated. But your program has helped her with her self-confidence. She's always telling us, 'Ms. Stacy said this, Ms. Stacy said that.' We're so grateful to God, we found you and CCA."

Her husband chimed in. "Anything you need from us, you just let us know." He reached down and picked up his daughter. "Let's get you home, dancing queen."

Kenzie giggled. "G'night, Ms. Stacy. See you tomorrow."

Stacy bid the family good night. As Arianna and her family drifted over, Stacy saw Cooper standing off to the side. His gaze, though less intense, didn't waver. She shook off the heat that crept up her face and focused on her senior student. She wrapped the teen in a hug. "You were outstanding tonight, Arianna. I'm so proud of you."

"Thank you," the young woman replied, beaming. "I really felt good out there tonight."

"I could tell. I see you caught the eye of a few our special guests."

Arianna nodded. "I got a couple of requests for auditions!"

"Excellent," Stacy replied. "I figured you would. We'll start working on some pieces for the senior showcase. You can use them for your auditions as well. I also want to commend you for how you turned things around with Kenzie. She was so excited that you took the time to work with her. You made her feel special, but more important, you helped her with her confidence. When you showed her that you believed in her, she believed in herself. She'll remember this for the rest of her life. I hope you will too."

Tears shone in Arianna's eyes. "Thank you, Ms. Stacy. I appreciate that."

"I'll see you tomorrow. Have a good night."

Toye slipped over to Stacy's side. "You did it again, girlfriend. The evening was a smashing success. We don't have the final tally, but I'm pretty sure we set a record for the silent auction."

"Thanks to Mr. Moneybags over there," Stacy said, frowning. "He's been staring at me all night."

"And why shouldn't he? You look fabulous. And if you play your cards right, you may get more than you know." She laughed at Stacy's horrified expression. "For CCA! Look, you can't avoid him all night. At least go over there and thank him for his generosity."

"Can't I just send him a note?"

"Go talk to him. And while you're at it, see if his friend is available. He's hot."

❧ ❧

"Relax, Coop," Eric said. "She's coming this way. Now's your chance. Just be your handsome, charming, rich self," he added, chuckling.

Cooper straightened his jacket. He hoped his smile did not convey the way his heart was beating in his chest. Her very presence sent his pulse racing. He extended his hand. "Ms. Roberts, I want to congratulate you on a successful event. I haven't had such an enjoyable evening in a long time." The electricity he had felt earlier had not diminished. In fact, it had only increased.

Stacy raised an eyebrow. "Really? I'm surprised. Based on your social media, I'd have thought your tastes would have leaned towards more, shall we say, high-brow performances."

Busted. "I've been known to attend my fair share of these types of events. It's always encouraging to see young people participating in such a positive endeavor. I'm glad Eric talked me into coming."

"More like twisted your arm," Eric said, shaking Stacy's hand. "I'll admit, I wasn't sure what to expect, but Cooper's right. This was a most entertaining evening. And Twila Dee was fantastic. I'm a huge fan. Do you think I could meet her?"

Stacy ignored the fake punch Cooper gave his friend. "I don't see why not." She looked over the men's shoulders. "Here she is now." She waved over Twila and her band members. Stacy shook hands with everyone and thanked them for their performance. After hugging Twila, Stacy introduced her to the waiting patrons. "Twila, I'd like you to meet Dr. Eric Woodson and Mr. Cooper Banks."

"It's nice to meet you both," Twila said. "Did you enjoy the performance?"

"Are you kidding," Eric said. "You're even more impressive live than on your CD. Would you mind taking a picture with me? I know some folks at work who will be dying to know I got to hear you perform tonight."

As Eric pulled out his phone, Stacy motioned for Cooper to step away. "Mr. Banks."

"It's Cooper, please."

She nodded. "We're grateful again for your donation of the NBA floor seats at the United Center. Apparently, they were a hot item. Maybe not because of the Bulls, but for the chance to see LeBron or Steph Curry in action."

"You're very welcome," Cooper replied. "I'm always happy to donate to a worthy cause."

"So it seems." She pulled out the bid sheet from her clutch. "Most of the bids were fairly reasonable, but $25,000 for a dance lesson is a bit much, don't you think?"

"I wanted to get your attention."

Irritation caused her to lose her smile. "I'm not for sale, Mr. Banks, at any price."

Now it was Cooper's turn to frown. "What makes you think I need to buy you? I wanted a dance lesson with you, and I wanted to make sure I got it."

"By putting up a fake bid?"

He reached into his jacket and pulled out a check. "There's nothing fake about my money. Or my bid for your time and training."

Stacy's irritation grew. Cooper was one of *those*: rich, smug, controlling. She'd been there, done that. Eric and Twila came over. "As I said, thank you for generosity, Mr. Banks. Dr. Woodson, thanks for coming and supporting us. Twila, let me walk you out. I'm sure your band is waiting for you. Have a good night, gentlemen." She turned on her heel and headed out the door with Twila and Toye.

"Well?" Eric asked. "How did it go?"

"It didn't." He held up the check. "I think I offended her."

"With your money?"

"Yeah."

"What now?" Eric asked.

"I have a better idea," Cooper said.

EIGHT

Stacy paused by the reception desk where her mother sat. Rose was the world's greatest office manager. She kept the schedule for all the students and teachers, took payments and greeted everyone by name as they came in and out the door. Stacy was amazed. Her loving spirit hadn't wavered since Stacy's childhood, even while living with her abusive husband. She infused the entire studio with her presence. From the children to the staff, everyone called her "Mama Rose." She made everyone she met feel like family, which was exactly the way Stacy wanted CCA to feel. "Busy day," she said.

"No busier than usual," Rose responded, smiling.

"Do you know how we did last night?"

Rose shook her head. "Toye is still reviewing everything with the finance team. But from what I hear, with that sizeable donation from that handsome Mr. Banks, we more than met our goal this year."

"How did we do without that donation?"

Rose frowned. "Why? What did you do?"

"I turned it down."

"You did what?"

Stacy shifted on her hip. "He thought he could use his money to buy my attention."

"He bid on a dance lesson that you offered in the auction," her mother replied.

"He bid ten times as much as the highest bidder on anything in the auction." Stacy shifted again. "Men who have money and power think they can do whatever they want." She blinked as memories began crowding her mind. "I've been there, done that. I'm not doing it again."

Rose sighed. "Oh, baby. I know what you've been through. But not every man is like that. There are plenty of good men out there, even the rich ones."

Stacy rolled her eyes. Her mother was the eternal optimist. "I'll take your word for it, Mama. I know we could have really used the money, but it was completely inappropriate. I'm sure if he really needed a dance lesson, he could afford any number of experts."

Rose pursed her lips. "I wish you had told me this earlier."

"Why? What did you do?"

"He called this morning," Rose said. "He said he won the lesson and he needed to get in as soon as possible. You had an opening this afternoon, so I put him on your schedule."

Stacy groaned. "Call him back and reschedule. Better yet just cancel it altogether."

"Is there a problem," a warm baritone echoed over shoulder.

Stacy stiffened. She hadn't heard anyone coming up behind her. Forcing a smile, she turned to see Cooper standing there, a mischievous grin on his meticulously bearded face. "Mr. Banks. It's nice to see you again."

"I'm going to pretend that you actually mean that instead of what you just said."

She resisted the urge to roll her eyes. "After last night, I didn't expect to see you. I'd like to apologize if I came off as rude or ungrateful."

"No apology necessary. I thought about what you said last night. That bid was way out of line. I confess, I'm used to certain kinds of women who prefer grand gestures."

"You mean they are into you for your money."

"Exactly." He reached into his jacket and pulled out a check. "I'd still like to give you the money for the bid." Before she could object, he added, "Consider it a donation to CCA. I was truly impressed by what you're trying to do here for our youth. Please accept this, with my deepest apologies for offending you."

He held out the check, but Stacy didn't take it. Instead, Mama Rose stood up and grasped it out of his hand. "I'll take that," she said. "And on behalf of everyone at CCA, we gratefully accept and say thank you." She shot her daughter a look.

Stacy scrunched up her face in response. "Thank you for your generosity, Mr. Banks. We will put your donation to good use."

"I'm sure you will," Cooper said.

"Mother, please make sure to give Mr. Banks a receipt before he leaves."

"I'll have your receipt ready after your lesson," Rose replied.

"Lesson? Mr. Banks—"

"It's Cooper."

"I'll accept the donation, but you don't have to take the lesson."

"But I want the lesson. I came prepared," Cooper said. He reached into his coat pocket and pulled out his wallet and handed Rose a black American Express card. "I believe you said the hourly rate for dance lessons was forty-five."

"Thank you," Rose said. "I'll add that to your receipt when you're done." She nodded her head in her daughter's direction.

"Fine," Stacy said, "follow me." She turned and headed down the hall. "It's safe to assume you're not here for a lesson in ballet, tap, or hip hop, not dressed like that."

Cooper glanced down at his attire. He had opted for a simple black sports coat and black jeans with a white shirt and silver and black tie. A pair of polished black ankle boots were on his feet. He wanted to come off as casual, yet professional. Somehow, he still managed to irritate the instructor. "No, actually I was hoping you'd teach me how to waltz."

She stopped and turned to face him. "Waltz? Are you serious?"

He nodded. "Every now and again, I must attend these affairs and there's dancing, the formal kind. Most of the time, I manage to avoid it, but occasionally I get caught. I'd like to learn how to dance without embarrassing myself or literally stepping on anyone's toes. You *do* know how to waltz, don't you?"

She raised her eyebrows and frowned in disgust. "Of course, I do. It's not complicated. You just have to be able to count to three. You *do* know how to count to three, don't you?" She didn't wait for his response but turned and entered an empty studio.

Cooper was impressed. The studio, though small, was open and clean. There were photos of dancers around the wall, some of which he recognized: Mikhail Baryshnikov, Alvin Ailey, Fayard and Harold Nicholas, Debbie Allen, Misty Copeland, Gregory Hines, Kathryn Dunham, Judith Jamison, and Stephen "tWitch" Boss. He was impressed that there was representation from multiple dance genres. One side of the room was covered in wall-to-wall mirrors, with a barre stretched across. A piano stood in one corner, and an older Bose music system was on a table in the opposite corner.

Stopping in the middle of the room, she turned to face him. "Have you had any dance training or experience?"

"Not unless you count the Electric Slide or the Cupid Shuffle at wedding receptions."

She rolled her eyes. "Well, at least you're familiar with moving to a beat. A waltz is a dance that moves in three-four time, meaning instead of moving at one, two, three, four, you only move on one-two-three in a basic box step." She turned and faced the mirror. "I'll demonstrate and explain at the same time. Take one step forward on your left foot, one step on your right foot to the right, then close with your left. Then back with your right, one step left then close to with your right." She demonstrated the movement a couple of times. "It's your turn." She positioned him at her side, so they were both facing the mirrors. "Here we go."

As they moved side by side, she could see him counting silently. It tickled her to see someone who came across so bold and confident move as tentatively as some of her six-year-old students. "You did good."

"That was terrible," Cooper said.

"That wasn't bad for your first time. You caught on quickly. But you need to loosen up. Give me your jacket and tie." She stifled a shudder as she watched him loosen the tie and unbutton the top buttons of his shirt. She pushed the thought of ripping off his entire shirt and rubbing her hands over him to the back of her mind. She resisted the urge to sniff his clothes, though the earthy musk scent that emanated from them only heightened her senses. She took a moment to center herself. *Focus on the dance. Focus on the dance.*

She crossed back over to where Cooper was standing. Forcing a smile, she said, "Okay, we're going to add arms. Do as I do." She positioned her arms as if she were the male lead, allowing Cooper to do the same. They began the box step again. As they did so, she couldn't help noticing Cooper had his eyes on her reflection in the mirror. She tried to focus on her own reflection, but the intensity of his gaze drew her in.

Shaking off the goosebumps the rolled up her spine, she turned to face him. "It's time for us to partner up. Are you ready?"

NINE

I am not ready.

Cooper could feel his heart racing and it wasn't from the dancing. It was unnerving having Stacy standing right next to him as he learned the dance. He couldn't help but stare at her as she walked away from him to put his jacket away. He tried to keep his expression neutral as he watched her moves in the mirror. Every step she took, every sway of her hips contributed to his growing desire.

Now, she was standing in front of him, face to face. He noticed tiny beads of sweat rolling from her neck down under the top of her leotard. How he wished he could see where they were going and where they ended up. He knew the steps by heart, but he kept his eyes downward, sure that if she could see his face, his innermost thoughts would be exposed.

"Mr. Banks?"

He looked up, surprised at how close she was to him. She smelled of vanilla, shea butter and coconut oil, a combination which left him thirsty with desire.

"Cooper? Are you ready to try this together?"

He swallowed, then nodded. She walked over to the stereo then programmed it. As she crossed the floor, the opening strains of Deniece Williams' "Silly" began to play. Before he knew what was happening, Stacy was in his arms, one hand clasping hers, the other on her upper back. He fought the urge to move his hand down toward her backside. He involuntarily shuddered when she placed her hand on his shoulder and moved in closer. She began counting out the beat and they began to move. Suddenly, she stopped and cut the music with the remote. “What are you doing,” she asked.

Cooper shrugged. “I thought I was dancing.”

“By staring at your feet?”

“Was I?”

She placed a finger under his chin and lifted his head, so his face met hers. “Part of the art of dancing is the connection with your partner. You are the lead. You must tell me where to go with your movement, with your body, and with your eyes. You can’t truly engage in the dance if I can’t see your eyes.”

As they resumed the dance, Cooper did his best not to physically react. Stacy’s touch had raised his senses to their peak but staring directly into her dark brown eyes sent him over the edge. He could see his future in them, a future that he knew he wanted, and not just with anyone. He wanted it with her. Every moment of his life had led him to this place...to Stacy. He whispered a silent prayer of thanks to God.

“Ow!”

Cooper was startled from his thoughts. “You okay?”

“You stepped on my foot,” Stacy said, grimacing.

“I’m sorry. I guess I wasn’t paying attention to my steps.”

“That much is clear.” She clicked the remote and the music stopped. “Our time is up.”

“Already?” He glanced at his watch. How had an hour flown by so fast? He knew in his spirit if he let her get away, they’d both regret it. “I don’t suppose I could buy another hour of your time to continue our lesson.”

He saw her stiffen. “Mr. Banks, I’ve humored you because of the auction and your generous donation. But if you are really interested in taking dance lessons, I can recommend several excellent instructors who would be more than happy to provide you with private instruction. Now, if you'll excuse me, I've got real students to teach." She spun around and left.

Cooper watched as she exited the studio. The last forty-five minutes had been the most exhilarating of his life, and it had nothing to do with his dance lesson. The connection they had was palpable. He didn't know exactly what he did to irritate her, but he was determined to fix it. "Our dance isn't over, Stacy," he said.

TEN

"Coop? Are you listening to me?" Eric's voice rang through the speaker.

"Sorry, man," Cooper replied. "I was distracted."

"Yeah, I can tell. It's that woman, right?"

"What woman?"

"Don't play dumb," Eric replied. "The woman from the gala—Stacy."

Cooper nodded even though his friend couldn't see his face. For the past three days, Stacy was ever present in his thoughts: the way she looked, the way she carried herself as she moved, every curve from head to toe, how she smelled of lavender, vanilla and coconut, how her very touch seared his soul. All he knew was he had to see her again. "Yeah, she's been on my mind."

"You're really hung up on her, aren't you?"

"There's something about her, Eric. Most of the women I've dated have been so caught up in my money and what it meant for their status. With Stacy, it's the exact opposite. It's as if my money repels her somehow."

"It's not your money, dude. It's the way you came at her. You were trying to be this big baller to impress her."

"That was your idea!"

"Which clearly didn't work. You need to come at her a different way."

"What do you suggest?"

Eric thought for a moment. "What's the one thing you know she's passionate about?"

"Dance. And Chi City Arts," Cooper answered.

"Exactly. Maybe if she sees that you'd like to help CCA, that could be your way in."

Cooper nodded again. "That's a good idea. You know, you're pretty smart sometimes."

"That's why they pay me the ridiculous bucks," Eric said, chuckling. "Gotta run and check on some patients. Let me know how it goes."

"I will," Cooper said. "Go heal some kids."

"I'm just an instrument of the Master Healer," Eric said.

"I hear that." Cooper hung up, then leaned back in his chair, fingers drumming on his desk. He mulled an idea around his head, thinking of the best way to approach it. He didn't want to alienate Stacy, but he sincerely wanted to help her and CCA. He needed to arm himself. He pressed the speed dial for his personal assistant.

"Hey boss. What can I do for you," Felicity Michaels asked.

"I need you to do some research on Chicago City Arts. Get me everything you can find on the organization—mission statement, founders, financials."

"Thinking of adding it to the portfolio?"

"Not sure yet. Maybe getting them aligned with the foundation."

"What's the timeframe," Felicity asked.

"Sooner is better."

"I'm on it," Felicity replied. Cooper hung up, then opened a new tab on his laptop. He googled Stacy Roberts. The initial search yielded several articles related to CCA and links to videos of past gala performances. As he scrolled, he came across a video of Stacy dancing solo, but the name on the video was simply, "Anastasia 2010." He clicked on the video. He was mesmerized by a younger version of Stacy dancing in a fiery, sensual performance.

When it was over, he did another search for "Anastasia dancer." He came across an article in *Dance Magazine*, heralding the rising star of Anastasia Cross. Described as gifted beyond words, she was destined for a long career on stage. He did another search for Anastasia Cross, but there were no follow up articles in *Dance Magazine* or anywhere else. Other than the video, there was no information connecting Anastasia Cross to Stacy Roberts.

"That's odd," he muttered. If Anastasia and Stacy were indeed the same woman, how did one go from the top of the dance world to running a financially struggling center on the south side of Chicago?

❧ ☙

"Chi City Arts, how may I help you?"

"Stacy?" He wasn't expecting her to answer the phone. "This is Cooper Banks."

She stifled a groan. "Mr. Banks. What can I do for you today? Surely you don't need another dance lesson."

"No, I'm good thanks. I'm surprised you're answering the phones."

"Mother had to step away, and everyone else is working. I'm not above answering the phones."

"I didn't mean to offend you," Cooper said.

Stacy sighed. "I'm sorry, Mr. Banks. It's been a long day. How can I help you?"

"No apology necessary, and please, call me Cooper."

"How can I help you," Stacy asked again.

"The reason I'm calling is I wanted to discuss partnering with you—with CCA, I mean!"

"Partner? I don't need a partner."

"Let me rephrase. I'd like to become a supporter of CCA."

"Why?" Stacy asked.

"Because I believe in CCA," Cooper said. "The MBIY Foundation, which I run, supports several youth organizations financially. I'd like to help support CCA. Unless you're financially solvent and have the resources you need to build the new facility you are promoting on your website."

Stacy paused. The new studio was a dream of hers, delayed only by financing. Cooper's offer was tempting, but she could not ignore how she felt when he held her in his arms as they danced, the electricity that pulsed through her as he stared into her eyes. Despite his inexperience, they moved in sync as if they had been dancing together for years. The idea of drawing even closer to him sent warm shivers down her body.

"Stacy? You still there?"

"Yes... uh, I'm here." She shook herself. *Focus.* "You said your foundation would like to support us. I'd like to hear what you have in mind."

"Great. Can we meet for dinner? Cooper's Hawk at eight?"

"No. I mean, I can't do dinner. Let's meet for lunch tomorrow. I'm free at 12:30 if that works for you."

"As it happens, I am. Do you like Italian? There's a great restaurant downtown called Volare."

"Italian is fine.

"Great. I'll make a reservation. I look forward to meeting with you," he said.

"See you then." She hung up the phone. "What am I getting myself into," she muttered.

"What's that?" Mama Rose said, hanging up her jacket.

"That was Cooper Banks. He wants his foundation to support CCA."

Rose clapped her hands. "Oh, praise the Lord! I knew that young man was the answer to our prayers."

"Hold on, Mama," Stacy said, switching places with her mother. "I haven't agreed to accepting anything from him. And even if I accept, we don't know what conditions he's placing on his help. His terms may require more than I'm willing to give." She blinked away tears as a rush of emotions threatened to overwhelm her.

Rose reached across and took her daughter's hand in hers. "He's not *him*, Stacy. Cooper seems like a good man, and he wants to help us. You can't allow your past to destroy a chance at something wonderful."

"But how do you know he's a good man, Ma? You don't even know him. I made that same mistake believing in a 'good' man once before. You know how that turned out."

"Yes, I know. And you've paid for those mistakes. But you're not the same woman as you were back then. You're both stronger and wiser. And we have the Lord on our side. I've been praying about this, baby. And the Lord has shown me that Cooper is the answer to our prayers. I believe it."

"I wish I could believe it too, Mama."

"I'll believe it for both of us, how about that?" Rose smiled. "Ask the Lord for wisdom and he'll give it to you, baby. Now go on, you've got a class to teach." Rose began greeting the first students of the afternoon as they entered the building.

Stacy smiled as she warmly greeted her students, but her thoughts were on Cooper and her mother's words. 'The Lord has shown me that Cooper is the answer to our prayers,' Rose said. *But which prayers?*

ELEVEN

Toye pulled up in the driveway of Stacy's condo. She grabbed her purse and bag from Mariano's Market, then headed to the door. Before she could ring the bell, Stacy opened the door and greeted her friend with a hug. "Careful," Toye said. "I brought wine. From the way you were talking this afternoon, you sounded like you need this."

"Great," Stacy replied. "I've got spaghetti Bolognese on the stove. Garlic bread is just about ready to come out of the oven." She stepped aside to allow her friend inside.

Toye loved coming to her friend's home. The varied hues of blue, silver and purple created a dynamic but warm space. Most of the wall was covered with lithographs of dancers Stacy admired. Upstairs, there were two bedrooms and a loft space that Stacy had converted into an exercise-slash-dance studio. It was one of the reasons Stacy never seemed to gain weight, despite her carb-heavy diet. "What's up, sis? Why the 9-1-1?"

"I'll explain over dinner," Stacy said.

The women sat for their meal and Stacy relayed everything that had transpired between her and Cooper, including his earlier phone call.

"I don't understand what the problem is, Stace. A rich, handsome man wants to give you the money you need to build your dream facility. This is a win-win, right?"

Stacy took another sip of her wine. "Maybe. But I've been drawn in by his type before. Look where that left me."

"First of all," Toye said, "Cooper is not Vincent."

"How do you know?"

"Because I did my homework. I checked him out."

"Toye!"

"As your best friend, your lawyer, and a member of your board of directors, I had to." Toye winked. "I didn't do it personally. I had my intern do it. Everting I've learned says he's the real deal. The worst thing any of his exes have said is that he's too nice."

"Exes. Plural," Stacy said.

Ignoring her, Toye continued. "Second, he's trying to do legit business with CCA. It's got to pass the smell test with the board. Since I'm on the board, if there's anything suspect about him and what he's trying to do, I'll find it out and he's dismissed."

Stacy nodded. More than being her best friend, Toye was one of the sharpest lawyers in the city. If anyone could find evidence of wrongdoing, she would.

"Third," Toye continued, "you are not the naïve, innocent teen that got sucked in by Vincent. You know better. The Holy Spirit gives us insight and wisdom. Trust Him if you can't trust yourself." She took her friend's hand. "You've got this, girl. If this man is who I think he is, your life is about to be changed forever." She stood. "Let's go pick out a killer outfit."

Cooper stood as the hostess led Stacy to his table. He took in the black knit pantsuit that accentuated her form. She kept the jewelry elegant, but simple, with a long silver chain that came to rest on her on her chest. A pair of silver earrings dangled from her lobes. Her hair was pulled into a loose ponytail, with a few strands hanging on the side. She'd opted to keep her makeup as natural as possible, with only a hint of color on her eyes, cheeks and lips. Those lips. He desperately wanted to taste her luscious lips. *Focus, Coop. Keep it professional.*

"Stacy, it's good to see you again. I'm glad you could make it. I hope you found the restaurant okay."

She smiled. "No trouble at all. I took an Uber. I hope I didn't keep you waiting."

"Not at all," Cooper replied. "I've only been here a few minutes." In truth, he'd been sitting there for a half hour. He slipped a generous tip to the hostess to seat him early and to keep the waitstaff from disturbing him. He needed the time to settle himself. Normally, business lunches were nothing new for him, but this meeting had so much more at stake. "Would you like to order a drink?"

"Just water, please."

Cooper signaled for their waitress. "Two sparkling waters, please."

The young woman nodded. "Are you ready to place your order, or do you need a few minutes?"

"I'm ready if you are," Stacy said. Seeing Cooper's surprised expression, she said. "I always research the menu to a new restaurant to find out what I might like."

"Good to know," Cooper said.

"I'd like the kale salad and the fattoria risotto, please," Stacy said.

"Very good," the waitress said. "And for you, sir?"

"The kale salad and I'll have the chicken diavola, please."

"I'll get your order started," the waitress said, excusing herself.

"You didn't even look at the menu," Stacy said.

"I eat here often," he replied. "I have my favorite dishes, but everything here is delicious."

"Lots of business lunches, I suppose."

"And dinners.

"With dates?" Stacy's eyes grew large as she clamped a hand over her mouth. "Oh, my goodness. I'm so sorry. I apologize. I don't know where that came from. That's none of my business."

Cooper chuckled. "It's fine. No, I haven't brought any dates here. Sometimes I come here for dinner when I don't feel like cooking. My condo is not far from here. I like the atmosphere and even though I'm dining alone, I like to people watch. I'm weird like that."

She smiled. "I don't eat out a lot. After spending my days with my students and dealing with staff and parents, I enjoy the solitude. If I want company, I may have dinner with my mom or Toye."

"Toye?"

"My best friend. She ran the auction at the gala."

He nodded. "I remember her. As I recall, she made quite the impression on my friend, Eric."

"I remember him. He's a doctor a Lurie's, correct?"

"Yes. He's a pediatric neurosurgeon."

"Impressive." She hung her head down and began giggling to herself.

"What's funny?"

She shook her head. "I'm ashamed to admit this, but when I met the two of you, I thought you were a couple. I told my mom that because she thought you were both so handsome. She was trying her not so subtle hand at matchmaking."

Cooper let out a laugh. "Wow! That's a first. Wait until I tell Eric."

"Please don't. I'm embarrassed enough as it is. In my profession, it's so easy to assume. Guess that will teach me."

"No harm, no foul. Maybe I'll let you make it up to me."

Stacy raised her eyebrows. "How?"

"Later. Our salads have arrived."

TWELVE

After the waitress set the food in front of them, he asked, "Do you mind if I bless the food?"

"Not at all," Stacy said, smiling.

Cooper took one of her hands in his. Ignoring the thrill that holding her hand did for him, he bowed his head and said, "Father, thank you for the food You have blessed us with, the resources to pay for it, and the bodies to accept the nourishment it will provide. Bless the hands that have prepared and served it. May we ever be mindful of those who are in need that we may be able to serve them. Bless Stacy, Ms. Rose, and our meeting today. In Jesus' name, amen."

Stacy echoed the amen and they began eating. "I'm curious. When did you start dancing," Cooper asked.

"Mama says I danced in her womb. From the time I could walk, I was dancing all over the house, so she put me in dance lessons, hoping to burn off some of that energy. I started at the Hyde Park School of Dance when I was four. When I was in high school, I did summers with Alvin Ailey and Hubbard Street. I even got a chance to dance overseas. By the time I turned eighteen, I had been accepted at a dance company and I was planning to dance professionally."

"What happened?"

A shadow fell across her face. "I injured my knee and ankle. I had to have surgery and rehab. I was told I wouldn't be able to dance professionally again. I was still young, so I pivoted. I went to Illinois State University, where I majored in dance education. You know they say those that can't do..." She chuckled wryly. Shrugging, she continued. "I minored in business because I knew I wanted to open my own studio. I did my student teaching and through their entrepreneurship program, I was able to secure a grant to start a dance studio in Normal."

The waitress brought their entrées and refilled their water. When she left, Cooper asked, "What brought you back to Chicago?"

She shifted in her seat, weighing her words carefully. "Mama. Her husband—my stepfather—died." Letting out a breath, she continued. "I came home to be with her. When I started CCA, she wanted to help. I couldn't afford to hire anyone, so she became my right hand. She helped me get organized, secure a location, you name it. She's as much CCA as I am."

"I've only met her once," Cooper said, "but she seems like a formidable woman."

"You have no idea," she replied. "Enough about me. I checked you out."

"I'm an open book."

"You made your first million by the time you were sixteen thanks to some incredibly fortuitous insight into the stock market. You graduated from Morehouse, earned an MBA from Northwestern. You've made every '30 Under 30' list there is. Own your own financial services firm. You've dated wannabe models and so-called influencers from coast to coast. Avid basketball fan."

"Guilty as charged."

"Where does the MBIY Foundation come from? I tried to google it but came up empty."

"It's a real thing," Cooper said, "if that's what you're wondering. MBIY stands for 'Minnie Believes in You.' It was named in honor of my grandmother, Minnie Banks. She was a philanthropist before people knew what that was. She cooked for people, housed them, sewed clothes, organized fundraisers, you name it. The one thing she truly loved to do was help young people. Minnie helped keep countless children in the community out of jail and gangs."

"She wasn't afraid of retribution?"

"Nope. She'd always say, 'Minnie Banks believes in you.' Those words empowered so many in her community. When she passed, the line was out the door of the church. So many came to share how those five words transformed their lives. I vowed that whatever fortune I made a portion would be used to create the foundation in her honor."

"But why keep it a secret?"

"Because I can't help everyone. Because there are scammers that take advantage of your generosity. My grandmother knew that, but she didn't care. I do. By keeping the foundation hidden, I can pick and choose those individuals or organizations I want to support after they have been thoroughly vetted."

"And you want to help CCA," Stacy said, her lips twisting.

"Yes."

"After one dance lesson."

"Not just the lesson. I heard what you said at the gala. I believe in what you're trying to do."

Stacy leaned back in her seat. "As much as CCA could use the funds, I'd like to hear more about what you're proposing."

"Fair enough." He reached into his portfolio and pulled out an envelope. "There are a lot of details to be worked through, but in short, I'd like to propose a partnership."

"Partnership? I don't need a partner." She threw her napkin in her plate and began to rise from her seat.

"Wait, please. Hear me out." Cooper waited until she settled back in her seat. "I don't mean it the way it sounded. I've done my research, too. Your biggest need is funding for your capital project—the new CCA studio and community center."

"That's right. We're about at capacity right now. If we can build a new studio, complete with a theater and production capabilities, we can expand our current programs, as well as provide a great community space for local artists to present their works."

Cooper nodded. "That's exactly what I want to invest in."

She leaned forward. "You want to build our building?"

"I do, but more importantly, I want to help you get the exposure you deserve. Not just for CCA, but for your students and those local artists you want to support. Like you did for Twila Dee."

"Twila is special. Her talent was evident from the first time I met her," Stacy said. "I connected her with a friend of mine who is an amazing voice coach. They recorded a demo, and she blew up. It was timing and opportunity, and she made the most of them."

He nodded. "That's what I'm talking about. You know there are more kids out there who just need the chance that you and Twila had. I'd like to be a part of that. Review the info. Talk it over with your board. I'll accept whatever you decide, but I'd still like to help. You set the terms."

Stacy looked at Cooper. The sincerity in his eyes matched what she heard him saying. Still, she knew enough not to walk into anything too good to be true with blinders on. She picked up the envelope. “Thank you for the lunch. I’ll read through this and take everything under advisement. I’ll be in touch.”

THIRTEEN

"He wants to do what?" Mama Rose exclaimed. She was serving dinner to Stacy and Toye, listening to her daughter recount her lunch meeting with Cooper.

"Not him, exactly, his foundation," Stacy said, buttering a corn muffin. "I know he's rich, but I don't think he's *that* rich."

"Oh, he is," Toye said, studying the proposal. "I checked. He could singularly finance the entire project if he wanted to. But, according to his proposal, the MBIY Foundation would be the primary capital funding partner and it would help CCA to source out additional capital." Toye looked up. "If we agree to this, we could have the new building built in two years, instead of five like we projected. And CCA wouldn't have to mortgage anything. Do you know what this means?"

"Spell it out for us, Toye," Rose said.

"CCA would have a brand new, state-of-the art facility debt-free! The only fundraising we would need to do would be for scholarships. We wouldn't even have to increase student fees. And it might be possible to give the staff raises," she said, winking at Rose, who clapped her hands.

"Oh, thank you, Jesus! Thank you, Jesus! I told you he was an answer to our prayers."

"Hold on, Mama. He's no savior. We've talked about this. We've been through this before. No one does something this generous without a price tag. From the looks of it, it's going to be a hefty one," Stacy said.

Rose took her daughter's hand. "Not every man is Vincent, or your stepfather. Don't let you past block the blessing God has for your now and your future."

"Mama Rose is right," Toye added. "He wants to do good for CCA and the community. Why not let him?"

Stacy pondered their words as she tore open the muffin and ate it. Her heart told her that her mom and best friend were right. Holding on to the past was costing her an amazing opportunity. But this time, she wouldn't just be opening herself to disappointment. CCA—and the future students they'd be able to help—might lose out. Yet, her head kept screaming for her to slow down and not fall so fast for the proposal this charming, and yes, handsome man had laid before them. This time, if it was a trap, her eyes would be wide open to see it coming.

"For the sake of the argument, let's assume he's serious about this proposal, no strings attached," Stacy began. "Would it be too much to ask for him to connect us with some long-term financial partners? It would mean more scholarships, equipment purchases and upgrades."÷

"I like how you're thinking," Rose said, laughing.

"Not to mention the free publicity for us and good public relations for them," Toye added. "It's a win-win for everyone."

"Think the rest of the board will go for it?" Rose asked.

"They'd be crazy not to," Stacy said. Her cell phone rang. She hid a smile as she saw Cooper's number. She answered, "Good evening, Mr. Banks."

"Good evening, Ms. Roberts," Cooper replied. "Why the formality? Am I interrupting something?"

She smiled. "I was just discussing your proposal with some of our board members."

"Really?"

She giggled. 'I'm having dinner with my mom and Toye."

"Give them my regards."

"Will do."

"So," he drawled out, "what do your board members think of the proposal?"

"It's impressive," Stacy said. "We're excited about the idea of getting started with the new building. What is more interesting is the idea that you would connect us with other long-term funding resources."

"I'm more than happy to do that. I'm connected with several individuals and organizations that are interested in supporting the arts and programming in underserved communities. You are exactly their target demo, and they are willing to put their money where their words are. They'd love nothing more than to attach their names to a rising star or a prominent non-profit that is impacting the community," he said, chuckling.

"I hear that." Stacy looked at her mother and friend, who were grinning, giving her a thumbs up. "You'll have to present to the whole board, but I don't see how we could turn down your generous offer."

"Wonderful. I included the contact information for Felicity Michaels. She's my executive assistant. Let her know the date for the presentation to your board, and she'll make sure it's on my calendar."

"I'll give her a call Monday," Stacy said.

"Um…," Cooper began, "there's one other thing."

Here it comes. "What's that?"

"I'd like to take you to dinner."

"Why?"

"Why?" Cooper asked. "Why does anyone go to dinner? To eat," he said, chuckling.

"No," she replied, frowning. "Why are you asking me to dinner?"

"Because I want to get to know you better."

"In what way? Look, Mr. Banks, I'd like to get something straight. If your offer to help CCA is contingent on you and I getting together, then I'll respectfully have to turn you down. I don't expect you to understand, but I am not for sale at any price."

"I didn't…I'm sorry. I always seem to be offending you," Cooper said.

"No offense taken."

"Good. Then let me be clear, *Ms. Roberts*. I never confuse business and pleasure. My offer still stands whether you have dinner with me or not."

Stacy nodded. "Good. Thank you for the call. I'll be in touch." She ended the call and faced her dinner companions. "What?"

"What was that?" Toye asked.

"He asked me to dinner," Stacy replied.

"And you just shut him down like that?"

"No, I made it clear that it would be strictly business between us," Stacy said. She stood. "I need some air." She left the table and exited out to the patio.

Toye shook her head. "I've never seen her like this." She glanced over at the older woman, who sat with a smirk on her face. "What are you thinking?"

"Hand me her phone," Rose said.

FOURTEEN

"Hey Cooper!"

Cooper spotted Toye waving at him in the foyer of the church. "Hi Toye. Good to see you again."

"I'm glad you were able to make it," she said.

"Thanks for the invite. I'm always happy to be in the house of the Lord," he replied. He took in her expression. "What?"

"I'm surprised you remember me, considering you've only had eyes for Stacy since you first met her at the gala," Toye said, grinning.

"Am I that obvious?"

She held up her thumb and forefinger. "Just a bit." She put a hand on his arm. "I checked you out. You seem like a stand-up guy. Don't prove me wrong. She deserves better than that."

He nodded. "I'll do my best to live up to my reputation." As they walked, he said, "By the way, I remembered you from the auction, but you made an even bigger impression on my friend, Eric."

"Did I?" Toye smiled. "Tell him I said hello."

"Will do." He looked around. "Where's Stacy?"

"She'll join us later. Let's get to our seats. Mama Rose is waiting."

ঌ ৻

Mama Rose stood as Toye and Cooper walked towards their seats. "So good to see you again, Mr. Banks."

"Good to see you too, Mama Rose," Cooper replied.

"And thank you for coming a few minutes early. I wanted a chance to speak with you privately, without Stacy knowing."

"Of course."

She gestured for them to sit before she spoke. "What are your intentions with my daughter?"

Cooper choked on his own spit. Toye patted him on the back, stifling a giggle. When he regained his composure, he said, "Come again?"

"Mr. Banks."

"Cooper, please."

"I've been around long enough to know that generosity such as yours usually comes with strings attached. You've said there are none, yet you've asked my daughter out. I suspect you've used your foundation to try and get closer to her. So, I'll ask it another way: are you interested in helping CCA because we need the help, or are you using your money to get my daughter into your bed?"

Cooper nearly choked again, but he pulled himself together. Something in her expression told him she was deathly serious. "You are truly a straight shooter, Mama Rose."

"I don't believe in playing games, Cooper, especially when it comes to my daughter."

Cooper turned to Toye, who shrugged. "Stacy is my best friend. I suggest you answer Mama Rose's question."

He turned back to the older woman, who had not moved an inch. "Truth?"

"That's always best."

Cooper nodded. He measured his next words carefully. "Yes and no. Yes, I want to help CCA because I believe in what you're doing. Anything I can do to help keep a kid off the streets and doing something productive, I'm one hundred percent onboard."

"What about my daughter," Rose asked.

"I confess, the first time I met her, I was in awe. She literally took my breath away. And I won't lie to you. I want to get to know her, but I want it to be in an honorable way."

"Marriage?" Toye squealed.

"Maybe. I'd like to see where this goes if she's willing and the Lord says so."

Rose nodded. "That's good. I appreciate your honesty. I'm glad to know you're a man of faith. I am also a woman of faith but let me be perfectly clear. My daughter has already been hurt too deeply to imagine. I will not allow that to happen again. If you do betray her, you will live to regret it."

The look in Rose's eyes bore deeply into Cooper's soul. "Yes, ma'am. I understand."

"Good. The service is about to begin." She turned away as the lights dimmed and the congregation stood to their feet as the praise teem took to the stage.

He leaned over to Toye. "Where is Stacy?" he whispered.

"It's her ministry Sunday," she replied with a wink. "You'll see her soon.

☙ ❧

Cooper was sweating.

By the end of the first song, he had ditched his suit jacket and tie, opened the top button of his shirt and rolled up his sleeves. He had not been to a church so physically vibrant and present in years. His own church was much more sedate in their worship experience, which he enjoyed because it made the teaching word of his pastor resonate with his analytical brain.

The experience at Citadel of Hope was so much more…alive. That was the only word he could think of to explain it. The congregation was unashamed to shout, dance, run, or whatever they needed to do to express their love and thankfulness to the Father. The praise and worship leader was fired up as he entered the stage, and with all the energy he had, he led the crowd in several songs, each one longer than the last. Everyone seemed unwilling to let the Spirit in the sanctuary ebb.

Cooper sat as the video announcements played. Taking out his handkerchief, he wiped his forehead and neck. *It's a good thing I work out regularly, or I'd be dead.* He smiled at Mama Rose, who just patted him on his knee. Toye said, "It's a lot for a first timer."

He nodded. "I'm enjoying it, though."

The video announcements concluded, and the lights dimmed again. The stage was lit, and a man dressed in a dancer's white tunic and palazzo pants with a red sash around him walked out and took a seat. Cooper perked up as the first strands of "Alabaster Box" by CeCe Winans began to play. Hesitantly stepping on the stage, Stacy, dressed in her own colorful tunic and pants, stumbled her way forward, making strides forward and back, carrying a small box in her hands.

The man, who Cooper surmised to be representing Jesus, sat and watched, one hand outstretched, compassion etched on his face. As "Mary," Stacy knelt at his feet, pretending to pour oil on his feet, and wiping it with her hair.

Cooper stood, as did many others, as Stacy continued her dance. As the second verse began, Stacy rose and began dancing freely across the stage. From the look on her face, the lyrics seemed to resonate with her personally. Every twist, turn, and leap shone bright as she lost herself in the worship of the dance. Jesus stood and joined in the dance, sometimes mirroring her moves, other times lifting and spinning her in the air. The dance ended as Stacy picked up her box and Jesus surrounded her and then led her off the stage.

The entire congregation was on its feet again, lifting their hands and shouting praises to God. Cooper wiped his eyes as he took his seat. He had never been moved to tears by a dance performance, but what he witnessed touched his soul. For the first time, he had seen beyond Stacy's physical beauty. He knew it was her spirit that was drawing him in. He looked to Mama Rose, whose hands were upraised in worship. Toye was also visibly moved. He saw an usher with a box of tissues walking through the audience. He waved her over and grabbed a handful of tissues and handed them to Toye, who nodded her thanks.

A thought rose to his consciousness. Mama Rose said that Stacy had been hurt before. How and by whom? He felt anger bubbling to the surface at the thought of anyone hurting her. He would tear them apart with his bare hands.

Vengeance is mine. I will repay.

Chastened, Cooper whispered a prayer of repentance and refocused his mind and heart on the word the pastor was delivering.

FIFTEEN

The rest of the service passed quickly. The pastor's message on forgiveness was both amusing and sobering. Seeking forgiveness, the pastor explained, was not just about saying sorry, but it was about true repentance for unacceptable behavior and making a change for the better. The pastor also said that forgiving didn't mean forgetting. You could forgive someone for your own peace of mind, but you didn't have to excuse their behavior or allow that person to still be a part of your life. True forgiveness from Christ didn't absolve you of your earthly consequences. The word gave Cooper a lot to meditate on.

The service ended and everyone stood as the pastor said the final benediction. The crowd began dissipating as people greeted each other. "What did you think of the service, Cooper?" Mama Rose asked over the noise.

"I'm so glad you invited me," he replied. "I haven't enjoyed church this much since I was a kid."

"What's your church like?"

"Let's just say, it's different," he replied, smiling.

"And what did you think of our girl," Toye asked.

Cooper shook his head. "She was amazing. I've never seen anything quite like that. I mean, I've been to the ballet and dance productions. I even enjoyed the children at the gala. But what she did on stage today, I honestly don't have the words."

Toye put a hand on his arm. "You better figure them out. Here she comes."

❧ ☙

Stacy greeted the various members of the congregation, some she knew, others she didn't. She accepted their compliments humbly, giving thanks to God along the way. Some of her students ran up to her to give her a hug. She greeted them warmly, answering their questions.

"I want to dance just like you," one girl said.

Stacy smiled. "You keep practicing, and maybe one day you will."

A boy stood next to her. "That guy that was dancing. Is he gay?"

Stacy's eyes grew large. "Why would you ask that?"

"Cuz' guys that dance like that are all gay."

"That's not true, and even if it was, it's none of our business. Besides, a lot of men dance like that. There are professional football players that have taken dance, did you know that?"

Now it was the boy's turn to be shocked. "Are you serious?"

"I am. Many football players take dance classes to learn how to be more agile on the field. How do you suppose those guys keep their toes pointed to stay inbound for a touchdown?" She chuckled, then reached in her purse and pulled out a card with CCA's information. "Why don't you come check us out?"

"I don't want to do no sissy dance."

"There's nothing 'sissy' about dancing. If you're not interested in ballet, we have tap and hip-hop classes, too."

"Yeah?" The boy took the card. "I really like hip hop."

"If you come to the studio, bring this card, and you can get a free lesson to see if you like it or not." She winked at him.

"Cool, thanks." The boy ran off to tell show his parents and she moved on. She spotted her mother and Toye talking to… wait, was that Cooper? What was he doing at her church?

Rose came to greet her. "You were wonderful this morning. You truly blessed our souls today." She hugged her daughter, whispering in her ear, "I invited him. Be nice."

"I'm always nice," Stacy muttered. She released her mother then hugged Toye. She then turned to Cooper. "It's nice to see you again, Cooper. I hope you enjoyed the service."

"I did, very much so," Cooper replied. "I was telling Mama Rose and Toye that it's so different from where I attend. Your presentation was amazing. The man you danced with, is he a professional dancer also?"

Stacy shook her head. "No, he's a gymnastics coach. He and I co-chair the dance ministry here."

"Yeah, Rick is phenomenal," Toye added. "He and Stacy work so well together. Too bad his wife gets all weird when they're on stage together." She pointed a subtle finger in the direction of Rick and his wife having a tense confrontation.

"That has nothing to do with me," Stacy said. "Stop starting stuff, girl."

"I'm just sayin'…"

Stacy shook her head. "Thanks for coming today, Cooper. I'm glad you enjoyed the service. You're welcome to join us again anytime." She turned to her mother. "Are you guys ready to go?"

"Uh…," Cooper began, "if you don't have plans this afternoon, I'd like to take you out to lunch. I'm sure you must be starving. I know I am after that workout during praise and worship." He gestured to the other two ladies. "That invitation is for everyone."

"That's really nice, Cooper, but I don't think so," Stacy said.

"Of course, we'll come," Mama Rose countered. "Thank you so much for the invitation."

Stacy stifled a groan, but she couldn't hide her frown. "Mother, what are you up to?"

Rose feigned innocence. "The man is hungry, and he offered to take us to eat. What's wrong with that?"

"I know I could eat," Toye added. "Why don't we go to Josephine's?"

"Perfect," Rose said. "They have the best Sunday brunch."

Stacy started to object, but her stomach gave her away. She rolled her eyes as Toye snickered. "Fine. Let's go eat. Cooper, I'll text you the address and you can meet us there."

"Why don't you two go on ahead," Rose said. "I have to speak with the pastor about something."

"We can wait for you."

"No, it might be a while. You can go ahead and get us a table. You know how crowded they are on Sundays. Toye and I will be along shortly." Rose grabbed Toye by the arm. "Let's go talk to the pastor."

"See you there," Toye said, adding a wink.

Stacy shook her head. She knew her mother and best friend were up to something. Turning to Cooper, she said, "Shall we go?"

He nodded. "Lead the way. I'll walk you to your car, then follow you."

She paused. "Oh, that's right. We rode with Toye. Guess I'll have to ride with you. I assume you drove."

"I did," Cooper replied. "May I take your garment bag?"

"Yes, thanks." She handed him the bag, grateful to take a little weight off her hands. They walked through the sanctuary waving to people here and there. Stacy ignored the raised eyebrows from a few of her friends, mostly directed towards Cooper. They talked mostly about the service, sharing their thoughts on the message. Cooper was especially intrigued by her choice of music for the presentation. "Pastor has been doing a series on forgiveness. Rick and I worked on the dance for a few weeks. The song seemed the perfect choice for today's message."

"Absolutely," Cooper said. "The two of you danced so effortlessly together. Did you choreograph it yourself?"

"We collaborated. I wanted to share Mary's story but to also show that Jesus was so much a part of her life, walking in step with her, lifting her up and carrying here when she needed it most."

"Honestly, it moved me to tears," Cooper said. "I will never read John 12 again without thinking of your dance."

"I'm honored," Stacy replied. She stopped in her tracks when she saw the Range Rover Velar. "Whoa. You drove here in this?"

"Sure. Is that a problem?" he asked.

"I suppose not for you," she said. He opened the passenger door and allowed her to sit first. She sunk into the luxurious interior, awed by the sheer splendor of the SUV. He climbed into his seat.

"This is amazing, Cooper. It smells new."

"It is new, well relatively. I've had it for a while, but I don't drive it much."

"Why not?"

"I work from home a lot. When I need to get around, I hire a car service. It allows me to meditate and focus on what I need to do without the aggravation of driving."

"But you drove here today."

"Traffic's better on the weekends." He winked at her. "I was also secretly hoping to impress you." He started the vehicle, waiting as other cars went past him.

She laughed. "Consider me impressed." She ran her hand along the interior. Her jaw dropped. "Does this actually have a massage feature?"

"It does. Try it out."

She programmed the touchscreen, then moaned in pleasure. "Oh my gosh, this is heavenly."

He chuckled. "Enjoy the ride."

SIXTEEN

The line at Josephine's was out the door. "I was afraid of this," Stacy said. "Josephine's is popular for the after-church crowd on Sundays. We might have to wait a while to get in."

"We could always go somewhere else," Cooper offered. "I know a couple of places in Bronzeville that we might be able to get in if I call now."

"Maybe. I had my heart set on that chicken and waffles combo, though." She walked over to the hostess to ask for a reservation, when a tall, bearded man came up. "Victor!"

"Hey, hey, if it isn't my favorite dancing queen!" He enveloped her in a hug. "How're you doing, Stacy?"

"I'm good. How's your mom?"

"Running the kitchen staff crazy, what else." He looked over her shoulder, saw Cooper and extended his hand. "Aren't you Cooper Banks?"

Cooper smiled and shook his hand. "I am."

"I'm sorry," Stacy said. "Cooper Banks, this is Victor Hanes. Victor and his mom, Josephine, own this restaurant. Victor and Josephine helped us get CCA established here and they're one of our many supporters."

"Pleasure to meet you, man," Victor said. "I've seen your profile on *Black Enterprise*. I'm very impressed by you and what you've done."

"I'm the one that should be impressed," Cooper said. "You're responsible for helping CCA get off the ground. I appreciate your investment in our youth."

"It's my pleasure." He turned back to Stacy. "Mama Rose called and said you'd need a table. I got you. Follow me." He turned and led them to a corner table for two. "Your server will be with you momentarily."

"Uh… Victor, Mama and Toye are supposed to be joining us."

"Yeah, about that, she called and said she had a headache and was heading home, and Toye had work to do, so she asked me to get the two of you a table. Enjoy your meal." He winked at her then headed for the kitchen.

Cooper pulled out the chair for Stacy, who was shaking her head. "I knew she was up to something."

"Come again?"

"Mama. She told me she invited you to church."

Cooper nodded. "She said it was to make up for our disagreement. From the look on your face, I'm pretty sure you didn't know I was coming."

"Yeah, it was quite the surprise. Look Cooper, I didn't mean to hurt your feelings. I learned a long time ago to keep a clear head when it comes to men like you."

He leaned back in his seat. "Men like me? What does that mean? Handsome men? Strong men? Black men? Men who can't dance?"

She laughed. "I mean charming men with money and influence. I learned a long time ago to keep my eyes wide open when it comes to men like you. Men like you take advantage of vulnerable women, use them up, then discard them like trash. I won't allow myself to be that woman again."

He reached for her hand. The spark he'd felt before intensified into a fire that burned in his eyes. "And there are women, beautiful, sexy, smart women, who cozy up to you, say everything they think you want to hear, only to find out they have their own agenda. They use you until you are no longer useful to them. I've been there, done that. I'm not looking for a photo op. I'm not looking for someone who wants me for what I have."

"What are you looking for," she whispered, her voice thick with emotion.

He rubbed his thumb across her hand. "I am looking for my forever partner. I'm looking for the one that will dance with me in joy and hold me in sorrow. I'm looking for the one who will tell me the truth, even if it hurts. I'm looking for the one who will stand shoulder to shoulder with me through good times and bad. My success is her success and vice versa. I'm looking for the one whose heart I will hold as precious as my life, and she will do the same for me. That's who I'm looking for." He smiled, then leaned back in his seat. "Does that answer your question?"

Stacy pulled her hand from his, wiping a tear from the corner of her eye. "You're good. Man, you are so good."

"Do you believe me?"

"I believe you. I don't know if I'm that one. That's a lot to live up to," she replied.

"Why don't you let me be the judge of that," he said. The waitress came to deliver their menus. "I think we're ready to order." He nodded at Stacy.

"I'll have the chicken and waffles with a large, iced tea."

"Make that two." The waitress took their orders and left them alone. "I like you, Stacy. That's as plain as I can make it. I'd like to get to know you better, and if this leads to something, wonderful. If not, we can be friends."

I could not be just friends with you. "Tell you what: after you present to the board, and if they accept your proposal, you can ask me out."

"When is the board meeting?"

"Two weeks."

He groaned. "Fine. Two weeks. I'll present, they'll accept, and so will you." His smile reeked with confidence.

Stacy shook her head. "We'll see." *It's going to be a long two weeks.*

SEVENTEEN

Stacy took a sip of her coffee and stared at the portfolio on the table in front of her. She didn't need to read the proposal; she knew it backwards and forwards, having read it every day for two weeks. She tapped her fingers on the table, willing the butterflies in her stomach to settle down. Today was the day that the future of CCA would be decided. The board was going to vote to accept Cooper's proposal. Stacy had no doubt about that. There was no way they could say no to his generous offer.

What had her heart beating faster was what she was sure was going to happen following the meeting: Cooper was going to ask her out. Since their lunch meeting at Josephine's, Cooper hadn't said anything in response to her proposition. When she said it, she knew it was going to happen. What she didn't know is why she said it in the first place. Sure, Cooper was handsome, charming, kind, and rich. But she had been there, done that with Vincent, and she wasn't interested in repeating past mistakes. Yet, something about Cooper was different. They had chemistry. Their conversation after his visit to her church made it clear that he was connected to God in a much deeper way than Vincent ever was. Still, her mind warned her to be cautious before giving her heart away again.

Her phone pinged with the verse of the day. Smiling, she read Jeremiah 29:11 in the New Living Translation: *'For I know the plans I have for you,' says the Lord. 'They are plans for your good and not for disaster, to give you a future and a hope.'*

"Father," she whispered, "I know You didn't bring Cooper into my life as an accident, but to provide a future and a hope for CCA and our students. Let me stand back and let You do only what You can and will do. And whatever happens, You'll get all the glory."

My plans are for YOU, to give YOU a future and a hope, the Spirit whispered back.

Her breath caught and she set her cup down. She'd learned to accept the promptings of the Holy Spirit but had never heard Him speak so clearly. Before she could even utter another thought, the Spirit spoke again.

Trust Me.

Tears formed in Stacy's eyes. Vincent had uttered those same words and he had nearly destroyed her. Since then, she'd learned to lean on her faith and the counsel of her mother and best friend. And while she had faith, the word trust sent shivers down her spine. Now, the Spirit was asking—no, commanding her to trust again.

Trust. Me.

As the tears fell, she whispered, "I'll trust you, Father. With CCA, with my life, with my heart. No matter what happens, I'll trust You."

❧ ❧

A round of applause erupted from the conference room, as CCA's board meeting wrapped up. Most of the board members came by to shake Cooper's hand and thank him for his generosity.

Several of the people wanted to take selfies with Cooper, but Felicity quietly discouraged them, reminding them of the terms of the foundation's agreement. CCA and MBIY Foundation would release a joint statement. Any publicity stemming out the foundation's contributions would keep Cooper's name and photo out of it. Felicity did arrange for a group photo for CCA's archives.

Having been through this before, Cooper welcomed the enthusiastic response from the board. He was just as eager to start the process of building the new facility that would change the lives of many more children and ultimately reshape an underserved community in Chicago. However, the only person he truly wanted to speak with was Stacy. She was talking with Toye and another board member. Occasionally, she would look up and give him a glowing smile. He willed his mind to take a mental photo as he vowed to do whatever it took to keep that smile on her face forever.

The last of the board members exited, leaving just Stacy, Toye, and Mama Rose. "If I do say so myself," Cooper said, "that was a successful meeting."

"You don't know how many lives you're about to change, young man," Rose said, wrapping him in a hug.

"I'm very happy to be a part of this." He looked at the younger women and said, "We should celebrate. How about I take us all out for dinner this evening?"

Stacy side-eyed him. "All of us?"

"Sure," Cooper said. "I think it would be a great idea."

"I'll pass," Rose said, "but you young people should go out on the town. Raise a glass for me."

"Are you sure, Mama Rose?" Cooper asked. "I promise not to keep you out too late."

"I'm sure," Rose replied.

"What about you two. You game?"

"I'm down," Toye replied.

"I guess I'm in," Stacy said, shrugging. "Where should we meet you and what time?"

"I'll have a car pick you up around six, if that's okay," Cooper said.

Stacy was about to object, but Toye chimed in, "Perfect. You can have the car pick us both up at Stacy's. She'll text you her address."

"Great. See you this evening." Cooper leaned over and gave Rose a kiss on her cheek. "I want a raincheck."

"I'll hold you to it," Rose replied, grinning.

"Looking forward to this evening, ladies. If you'll excuse me," he said, walking to the door.

Stacy turned on her friend. "You didn't ask where we were going."

"He's sending a car for us, so I'm pretty sure it's not McDonald's," Toye said, laughing.

EIGHTEEN

"It's not a car," Toye exclaimed, "the man sent a limo!"

"Are you serious?" Stacy peeked out of her living room window. "This dude is too much."

"I like his style," Toye said. She grabbed her wrap and purse. "You ready to go?"

Stacy nodded. "Let's go."

Once in the limo, the ladies enjoyed a glass of wine, as instructed by the driver. "Where are we going?" Stacy asked.

"I'm not at liberty to say, per Mr. Banks' instructions," the driver said with a hint of a smile.

Glancing out the tinted windows, Toye said, "It looks like we're headed downtown."

Stacy nodded. "We're probably heading to Volare. It's his favorite restaurant." Seeing her friend's raised eyebrows and smile, Stacy laughed. "That's where we met for our lunch meeting."

The women chatted amiably until Stacy realized they had passed the exit to the restaurant. As the limo made its way north on DuSable Lake Shore Drive, they could see the lights from the Centennial Wheel at Navy Pier looming in the distance. The driver pulled over at the entrance to the pier, got out and opened the door. A smiling Cooper extended his hand to assist them out of the vehicle and they were pleasantly surprised to see Eric joining them.

"I hope you don't mind me tagging along," he said. "Cooper told me the good news and asked if I wanted to join in on the celebration. How could I say no?" He eased up next to Toye. "Especially when we are in such lovely company."

Toye blushed. "It's nice to see you again, doctor."

"It's Eric, please"

"You can call me Toye."

Cooper rolled his eyes. "Ladies. Eric. We'll have to walk fast if we're going to make our reservation." He held out his arm to Stacy. "Shall we go?"

Nodding, she wrapped her arm in his and quickly felt the same electric sensation pulsing through her body from when they danced. She smiled as they quickly fell in step, grateful she had worn her low-heeled black leather pumps. The skirt of her purple tea-length dress swished around her legs as she walked. She was tempted to open her black wool cape but thought better of it. Though it was a mild for a night in early February, she knew the temperature by the lake could easily drop. When she realized where they were headed, she turned to Cooper. "You made reservations on the Odyssey," she said, glancing at the largest ship on the pier. "Why didn't you just make a reservation at Volare?"

"I thought tonight we should do something special to celebrate. I go to Volare all the time. I thought we could have a great meal, do some dancing, and enjoy the view."

"And what if I hate boats? What if I get seasick? What if Toye gets seasick?"

"I don't get seasick," Toye piped in.

"Do you get seasick?" Cooper asked.

"No, but it would have nice to be prepared."

"I'll keep that in mind for next time." He winked then led her aboard. After a quick pre-board photo, they stopped by the bar and picked up their drinks. They were seated on the upper deck near a window, giving them the perfect view of the lakefront in the evening. They toasted to CCA's new future and the partnership with the MBIY Foundation. After a sumptuous meal, the DJ began playing up-tempo music, encouraging the passengers to get on the dance floor. When he put on the "Cha Cha Slide," nearly everyone was up and dancing.

Stacy was surprised at Cooper's flair for the group dance. He seemed more relaxed than she'd ever seen. The four of them laughed as they tried to outdo each other doing all the moves. The next song was "The Wobble," followed by "Cupid Shuffle." By the time they were done, the guys had shed their jackets and were searching for some cold water.

"Whew, girl, I don't remember the last time I danced that long and hard," Toye said, mopping her forehead with a napkin. "Those guys were laying it down!" She looked at her friend. "Tell me again why you aren't out of breath?"

"I dance for a living, remember?" Stacy said, laughing. "I have to say though, it's nice to just dance and have fun, rather than teaching or performing." She fanned her hand in front of her. "I wish I had worn something a little lighter though."

"Girl please, you look fabulous," Toye said. "The only time that man took his eyes off of you was when he had to turn during the dance."

The men returned carrying glasses of water which the ladies gratefully accepted. The next song began to play and the familiar musical notes of "Silly" came through the speakers. "Think you could go one more round?" Cooper asked.

Stacy smiled. "Are you sure?"

Cooper nodded then took her hand and led her to the center of the floor. Positioning himself with her in his arms, he counted out the beat and began leading her in a waltz. As the song's notes ebbed and flowed, Cooper kept time, effortlessly leading Stacy around the floor, spinning her at various points. The rest of the passengers began to step back to give the couple room.

Stacy tried to focus away as she had been trained, but her eyes kept returning to Cooper's earnest gaze. She could tell he wasn't counting his steps but was fully confident in what he was doing. This moment was theirs. It didn't matter who was watching; she knew instinctively that he was declaring that she was his. *Oh love, stop making a fool of me.*

The song ended and the crowd erupted in applause and whistles. "Let's give it up for our dancing stars," the DJ said. "Take a bow!"

Cooper waved to the crowd, a huge grin on his face. Stacy curtsied lightly, then whispered, "Excuse me." She turned and made her way to the exit. As the DJ ramped up the music, Cooper walked towards Toye and Eric, accepting compliments along the way. Eric gave his friend some dap, saying, "Man, that was tight! You need to go on *Dancing with the Stars*."

"You both were amazing," Toye said. "If that's how good you got after one lesson, Stacy is a better instructor than I thought."

"Where did she go?" Cooper asked. "Did she go to the restroom?"

Toye shook her head. "She went in the opposite direction. I think she went up on the deck."

NINETEEN

Brushing away an errant tear, Stacy stared out at the lights of the city's beautiful skyline on the horizon. An involuntary shudder coursed through her body. The rational side of her brain knew she had no business standing in the cold, especially after working up a sweat on the dance floor. But she had to get away from the crowd to clear her head. She smiled, remembering how smooth the dance with Cooper was. It was a far cry from the awkward lesson they'd shared four weeks earlier.

As exhilarating as the dance was, it wasn't what was uppermost on her mind. Being with Cooper had reignited a fire inside her that she was sure had been extinguished after her disastrous marriage to Vincent. From the moment she met Cooper, the electricity that passed between them whenever they touched was something she thought she could ignore.

Tonight's dance changed all that. Every touch, turn, and look had electrified every cell in her body. His confidence extended beyond the steps. He was in control, yet he was gentle enough to guide her in each move so that it felt instinctual. As the dance floor cleared, Cooper felt stronger; it showed in every step. For a moment, it was just the two of them, the rest of the world fading away.

It wasn't just the electricity. Being on the floor, moving in time with the music reminded her of why she fell in love with dancing. The movement to the music was freeing. She could just *be*. In the moment, nothing else mattered.

She felt warmth around her body as Cooper came behind her, draping her wrap around her shoulders. "Thank you," she whispered.

"I can't have you out here catching your death of cold. Mama Rose would kill me," he said, chuckling. "Why did you run out?"

"Just needed some air," she replied.

He moved to face her then took her hands in his. "Why did you really run out?"

A whiff of his scent sent her electricity meter off the charts. She couldn't deny her growing feelings. "I needed to get away from you, Cooper."

"Did I do something wrong," he asked, frowning.

She shook her head. "You were fine. In fact, you blew me away with your dance skills."

"I had a great teacher."

"I'm good, but not that good, Cooper, not after one lesson."

Smiling, he said, "Busted. I've been practicing. I took a couple of extra lessons from a private instructor. And, you know, YouTube."

"And you had to show off in the most public place possible. For someone who values his privacy, you sure love public displays. How much did you pay the DJ to play that song?"

"Enough that every time he hears it, he'll have a smile on his face." He brushed a tear that escaped her eye. "What's wrong?"

"Nothing."

"Stacy, talk to me."

She brushed away another tear. "What do you want me to say?"

"Tell me what you're feeling."

"I don't know what I'm feeling."

"Try."

She sighed. "I feel happy. Scared. Confused. Alive. Terrified." She looked up at him. "I don't know what this is between us. I don't know if I can risk my heart again."

Cooper laid a hand on her cheek. "I won't hurt you, Stacy. With everything that's in me and God as my witness, if you let me in, I will guard your heart as if it were my own." He wiped another tear from her cheek.

"I want to believe you," she whispered.

"Believe this." He lowered his face towards hers, his lips brushing hers. He tasted the sweetness of her iced tea and the saltiness of her tears. When she didn't pull back, he deepened the kiss, his lips parting slightly. He felt her mouth open slowly, then wider, her arms wrapping around his neck, pulling him closer. Her tongue sought his and found it, hesitant at first, then eagerly moving together in a dance of their own. For the moment, nothing and no one else existed as the head of the kiss warmed them from the inside out.

Stacy pulled back abruptly. They both took several deep breaths, regaining their senses. "I'm sorry," he whispered.

"I'm not," she replied. Pulling him into an embrace, she rested her head on his chest. "That was nice."

He rested his chin on top of her head. "It was. Are you okay?"

She nodded in his chest, then burst into sobs. Wrapping her in his arms, he ran his hands up and down her back, trying his best to soothe her. He could hear her trying in vain to stifle her cries, even as her body convulsed. *Lord, I don't know what's wrong, but You do. Touch Stacy and heal her broken heart.* He waited as she calmed herself. He kept her close, hoping she was able to draw on his strength.

"I'm sorry," she said quietly.

"For what? I was already wet from dancing." That elicited a chuckle. "If I went too fast…"

"No, that's not it." She shuddered again. "There's something you need to know about me."

She looked up, her eyes locking with his, hoping he would not be repulsed by what she had to say. "I was married before. I was eighteen, and he was my benefactor. He was rich and powerful, and he promised me the world. I was going to be the next Misty Copeland, Debbie Allen, and Judith Jamison all in one. For a while, I believed him. He made sure I had the best clothes, trainers, nutritionists, masseuses. But all that came with a cost. He wanted control—of what I ate, where I went, who I talked to, what I wore. He didn't want me to associate with the other dancers in my company. I was to focus only on him and the choreography. When I wasn't at my best, if I was tired or sick, I was forced to dance, and he would belittle me in front of the company. He said it was to toughen me up to handle the pressures of being a superstar. If I wanted to hang out with my mom or Toye, he had to come along. If I complained, he'd hit me, but not where anyone could see the bruising." She laid her head against his chest again. "And when I was too tired for sex, he'd take what he wanted," she whispered.

Cooper stifled a curse, but a low growl rumbled in his chest. He didn't know this man who had hurt her so deeply, but if he ever did meet him, he might not be responsible for his actions. That was for another time. Right now, he needed to listen to the rest of her story. He wanted her to tell it however she needed to say it. "What else," he ground out.

"I was under so much stress, I began to lose weight, my hair began to fall out, I wasn't sleeping at night. I couldn't concentrate on my choreography. The worse I danced, the more vicious he became." She sighed. "Two days before our opening, I made a turn and I felt something pop in my foot and my knee. I fell, writhing in pain. I tried to get up, but the pain was excruciating. One of the dressers called Toye and she came to take me to the hospital. Turns out, I tore my ACL and broke a bone in my foot. After surgery, the doctor said I'd fully recover, but with all I had been through, he said I wouldn't be able to dance professionally again. I was devastated, but Vincent was enraged. He blamed me, said I was ruining his plans, that if I had been good enough, it wouldn't have happened."

"Bastard," Cooper muttered. *Forgive me, Lord.*

"He filed for divorce the day of the opening. Had me served with papers while I was in rehab. He locked me out of our apartment and took everything. If it hadn't been for one of Toye's mentors, I would have been stuck with the hospital and therapy bills. My lawyer convinced him to pay all my bills and in exchange, I wouldn't contest the divorce, I wouldn't come after him for spousal support, and I wouldn't expose his dirty secrets."

"Why didn't you go to the police when all of this was happening?"

"I was young and scared. I didn't think anyone would believe me, except mom and Toye. On the outside, he's as charming as they come. But alone, when no one is watching, he's a monster."

"Still..."

She pulled back and looked him in the eyes. "It's an open secret—what happens in the dance world, stays in the dance world. You can't publicly complain about the treatment you receive at the hands of a choreographer, creative director, or producer. Word gets out and suddenly you're blacklisted from companies, theater productions, auditions. I was an up-and-coming dancer with no clout. Vincent was everything. Had I spoken up, the repercussions would have been devastating. Keeping quiet earned me enough good will in the professional dance community to help me when I was starting over. I've been able to help my students earn college scholarships, as well as being placed in some of the best professional companies in the nation because I kept my mouth shut. For my kids, my silence was worth it. God has healed me and allowed me to move on with my life."

Cooper nodded, trying to settle his emotions. "Speaking of starting over, what about your name change?"

She ducked her head again. "Of course, you found out about that. I loved the name my mother gave me. As a dancer, it sounded so exotic. I envisioned becoming a one-name star, like Beyonce. But every time I heard him say my name, it literally made me sick. As soon as my divorce was final, I legally changed my name. Anastasia Cross became Stacy Roberts. I used my mother's maiden name. New name, fresh start."

"You shouldn't let him take your name. It's beautiful, like you," he said, stroking her cheek.

She pushed away as her eyes hardened. "He didn't take it. I gave it up. What do they call it? It's my 'dead name.'"

The look on her face told Cooper she meant business. He decided to change the subject. "Will you go out with me?"

"I'm sorry, what?"

He smiled. "We had an agreement, remember? You said if I convinced the board to accept my proposal, I could ask you out."

She smirked. "This isn't a date?"

"No, this is a celebration. I would never ask your best friend and mine to join us on a date. However, I suspect we may wind up on a double date at some point. Eric is really feeling your girl."

Stacy decided to keep that little nugget to herself. As she mulled over his question her mind and spirit waged a battle.

Don't go.

What's the harm?

He'll break your heart. Again.

No, he won't. Trust Me.

The Spirit won out. "Ask me again."

He straightened up, then looked her in the eye. "Stacy Roberts, will you go out with me?"

"Yes."

It was all he could do to keep from dancing all over the deck. "What are you doing Friday night?

She thought for a moment. "Nothing special. Just preparing for Saturday's classes."

"I'd like for our first date to be something special. Will you go?"

She shrugged. "I guess so."

TWENTY

"Of all the places to go on a first date, he had to pick a red-carpet charity event. We couldn't just go to Olive Garden?" Stacy asked her reflection.

With less than a week to prepare, she hunted down a dress online, rescheduled all her Friday classes and begged her hairdresser to squeeze her in. Seeing the results in the mirror, she knew she was red-carpet ready. The butterflies she was experiencing weren't about having her photo taken. They were only there because this was her first "official" date with Cooper.

She had been dreaming of their kiss all week. He called her every morning just to say hello and every evening to say good night and have a word of prayer. In between, there were texts about everything and nothing, and many more confirming the details of Friday night.

Snow flurries drifted outside her window. Anticipating the weather, she'd arranged for Cooper to have the limo back into her heated garage. He'd assured her that she wouldn't have to step out in the elements, which would have turned her soft waves into a curly beehive. She twirled in her full-length mirror, thanking God that the gown she'd rush ordered online fit her perfectly. Satisfied, she made her way downstairs.

❧ ❧

Cooper checked his watch. He'd arrived early, much to Stacy's dismay, but he didn't want to take the chance of being late for the red-carpet arrival. He wanted the world to know who Stacy was and he was the man lucky—no, blessed enough to end up with her. He knew it wouldn't stop the social media speculation about his love life. He didn't care. He only cared that the woman of his dreams—of his heart—would be on his arm tonight and hopefully forever.

He looked around Stacy's home and was pleased with what he saw—modern, stylish, artistic, cozy. The entire place felt like her—like home. *Maybe she'll do the same to our home.* He paused at the thought. *Our home.* The place he would buy for her, let her put her creative touch on. The home for them to love, laugh, and cry in, make love in, make babies in, grow old in. He didn't even know if Stacy could have children or even wanted them. It was a conversation they would have to have soon. Cooper knew he was meant to be a father; he wasn't about to invest his heart with someone who couldn't envision kids in their future. "Slow your roll, Coop," he whispered, "tonight's not the night."

A flash of red descending the stairs caught his eye and he stood. "I…"

Words escaped him as Stacy stood before him, a vision in blazing red. The silky crepe material fit her like a second skin, allowing her curves to be on full display. Toned arms at her side, with only a diamond tennis bracelet adorning her wrist. The lower half of the dress was a series of ruffles that floated in air, cut through by a split to one side, revealing one very muscular and sexy leg. A pair of strappy silver heels adorned her perfectly pedicured feet.

She cleared her throat, and he looked up to see her smiling. "You like?"

"You're so wrong," he answered huskily.

"What?" She looked around nervously. "It's not right?"

"No, you're wrong for making every other woman tonight look like they just rolled out of bed.

"You're silly," she said, giggling.

"And you're beautiful." He crossed over and pulled her close. "I don't know what I did to deserve you, but I thank God every day he brought you into my life." He cupped the back of her head and leaned in for a gentle kiss, loving the way the soft waves of her hair felt in his hand. She smelled of peach, vanilla, and musk. He loved the scent of it on her skin, not like the cloying overpriced fragrances some of the women he'd dated had insisted on wearing.

Smiling, he pulled back. "We should go." *Before I start something we can't finish. Yet.*

"I'm glad I'm wearing smudge-proof lipstick, or you'd have a problem, sir."

"I don't care," he said.

"You would if you saw yourself in red lipstick."

He chuckled at the thought, then turned and picked up her cashmere cape and draped it around her. Holding out his arm, he escorted her to the limo.

They settled in and he offered her a glass of sparkling wine. "Tell me something," he began. "I see you have a perfectly lovely garage with nothing in it."

"Are you asking if I have a car?"

"Yes."

"The answer is no," Stacy said. "I had a car, but it kept giving me trouble. I was pouring good money after bad, so I got rid of it."

"Why didn't you purchase another one?"

"My salary is not as much as you think. Besides my mortgage, I'm just finishing paying off my student loans. I don't want to take on another note yet. I ride with Mama to work and Toye and I ride to church together. Everywhere else, I take a rideshare or public transportation."

"Maybe tonight will change your mind about getting a new vehicle," Cooper said.

"Maybe, but I doubt it."

We'll see about that, Cooper thought, sipping his wine. He pulled out a brochure. "Before we get there tonight, there's something I've been meaning to tell you. You know the whole point of the First Look for Charity is that all proceeds are divided among several charities and non-profits."

She nodded as she took the flyer from him. Scanning it, she nearly dropped her glass. "How is CCA on this list? I've never even been to the auto show before, much less applied for this program."

"I know people," Cooper said, shrugging. "I know how this process works, so I made a few phone calls. Once I was committed to helping CCA, I decided to utilize every resource at my disposal. Whatever proceeds are generated from tonight, CCA will be getting a very nice check."

"Oh, Cooper," she whispered, a tear falling on her cheek, "you don't know what this means." She kissed him sweetly. "Thank you."

TWENTY-ONE

The entrance to McCormick Place was lit up in style. Stacy saw a few celebrities getting their photos taken. Athletes and actors with their spouses or significant others posed for photos before entering the hall. Stacy gripped Cooper's hand. "What's wrong," he whispered.

"I haven't been out in public like this in years," she replied. "What if someone recognizes me and asks questions?"

"Tell them the truth. You're Stacy Roberts, founder, and executive director of Chi City Arts. That's the story. That and that killer dress you're wearing." He tucked a finger under her chin. "This is about our first date. Relax. Have fun." He gave her a quick kiss, then escorted her on the red carpet. The media took their fair share of photos and asked simple questions about CCA and how she felt about participating in the charity event. Eventually, they moved on to the next person strutting across the carpet.

Inside, the atmosphere was dazzling. There were makes and models of every auto manufacturer, both foreign and domestic, featuring coupes, sedans, SUVs, and pickups. Every manufacturer had their own concept car on display, and the newest model ready to roll off the production line in the upcoming year. The couple had fun getting in and out of select models. Stacy really enjoyed the test tracks, riding around as the drivers showed off all the features of the vehicle they were in. She wondered how many times they had to repeat the spiel during the ten days of the show. As they made their way to the "super car" exhibit, Cooper asked, "See anything you like?"

"I like them all," she replied, "although that Jeep was definitely built for someone who spends time in the great outdoors."

"If you had your pick, which vehicle would you buy?"

She eyed him curiously. "Why?"

"It's just a game," he replied, his expression neutral. "You know, like what would you do if you won the lottery. Play along. If money was no object, what would you pick? Not just for yourself, but for anyone you wanted."

"Just a game, right?" She stopped. "Okay, let me see. Hmmm… a Mercedes Sprinter van for CCA. I'd have it retrofitted so we could load up equipment and costumes for outside engagements, instead of having to depend on parents to transport. When we're performing outside, we could use it as a power source for amps and speakers. The kids could use it to change instead of public restrooms. Ick."

"Nice. That's business. Let's get personal."

"Right. For Toye, the electric BMW. Black sapphire, fully loaded."

He nodded. "Why?"

"Because she'd never buy it for herself. She wants to save people and the planet. She does a lot of pro bono work, so she keeps her costs to a minimum. I suspect when she dies, she's going to have a multi-million-dollar endowment to leave her alma mater. Toye is frugal, except when it comes to vacations. Then she rides like a queen."

He laughed. "Cool. What about Mama Rose?"

Her smile widened. "Mama deserves something really nice after all she's been through." Cooper noticed a sadness in her eyes, but she continued. "I'd get her one of those S-class Mercedes coupes in red, with a white interior, wood trim, fully loaded."

"Why red?"

"It's her favorite color. Reminds her of the blood of Jesus," she said giggling.

"Is the white for being pure as snow?"

"No, the white because black leather in the summer is horrible!" They both laughed, each remembering their fair share of burned backsides on hot leather seats.

"What would you get for yourself?"

"Hmmm… the Lincoln Navigator."

That surprised him. "Really. Why?"

"I work with our dance team at church. A lot of the kids need rides home. I'd like to be able to transport them and still have room for costumes, equipment, whatever."

He stopped and put his hands on her arms. "I love that you'd want to use your vehicle to serve others. But what about something just for yourself? Something that you and Toye could ride around in and hang out? If you only had to think about yourself, be totally selfish, what would you pick?"

"Just for me? I don't know." She shrugged. "Maybe the Aviator with that full sunroof. I'd love to drive down DuSable Lake Shore Drive on a sunny afternoon with the roof open or just have the sun shining down on me with the tunes cranking."

He smiled. "I would have thought you'd go for something sportier."

She shook her head. "Small cars scare me. If you're in an accident, you'd get crushed like a pop can. I've always liked larger vehicles. Something about them just feels right. Plus, if I ever have a family, I don't want to switch from a tiny car to a minivan. The SUV works for me."

As they continued their walks through the exhibits, Cooper couldn't keep the grin off his face. *God, you're awesome! You answered my prayer before I even asked!*

❧ ☙

"I had a wonderful time tonight," Stacy said, snuggling next to Cooper in the limo. "All those beautiful cars, the music, the food…" Her stomach rumbled, causing her to chuckle. "Okay, it was tasty, but that was no real dinner."

"Hungry?" Cooper asked. "What do you have a taste for?"

"Honestly, I could go for breakfast. I think I'll make myself a sausage and egg sandwich when I get home."

"Nonsense," he replied. "You look too good in that outfit to end the night so soon. I have the perfect place in mind." He hit a button to speak to the driver. "David, take us to the Palace."

The "Palace" turned out to be the White Palace Grill, a twenty-four-hour diner just off the expressway. Even though it was almost eleven o'clock, the parking lot was nearly full. They entered and found themselves waiting in a brief line before the hostess seated them at a booth.

"We're a little overdressed for this place," Stacy whispered, perusing the menu.

"Maybe, maybe not. Your dress fits right in with the décor," he said, glancing around. Indeed, the gleaming red and white tiles surrounding the walls complimented the booths and chairs that were accented in red.

A waitress came by and placed glasses of water in front of them. "Coming in or going out?" she asked. "Either way, you class up this joint. What can I get you?"

Cooper ordered a Texas omelet and Stacy ordered a sausage and egg sandwich with a milkshake. The waitress took their orders and left. "She's right. You class up the place. Have I told you tonight you look amazing?"

She beamed, her eyes sparkling. "Yes, you have, but it never hurts to hear it again." She reached over and took his hand. "I don't know if I told you before how much I appreciate whatever it is you did to get CCA on that list of charities. That donation will go a long way in providing scholarships for so many students, not to mention it'll be a great jumpstart on our building fund."

"It was my pleasure." He pulled his hand to her mouth and kissed it, sending goosebumps racing across her entire body.

Pleasure is the wrong word. Try bliss, rapture, desire.

"Stacy?"

"Hmmm…" She noticed him staring at her, a cocky grin on his face. *Focus girl!* "What?"

"I said I want to ask you about something you said earlier."

"Sure. Ask away." *Ask me if I want you to kiss my hand again. Ask me if I want those lips on mine.*

"When we were pretending about cars, you said you wanted a vehicle to accommodate a family. Is having children part of your future?"

"That's not really a first date question, is it?" She added a laugh, but she saw the seriousness in his eyes. She nodded.

"I've always wanted children of my own. I knew it wouldn't happen until I retired from dancing professionally. I thank God every day that I didn't have one with my ex. The thought of being tied to him forever..." She shuddered. "Knowing him, he would have been completely disinterested in being a father, except to use it as a pawn to keep me under his thumb. Worse, he would have tried to turn him or her into his next project. The abuse that child would have suffered..." She shook her head. "I would have killed him if he ever hurt a child of mine."

Cooper knew she was deadly serious. He didn't know her ex-husband except for the little she had told him. He couldn't imagine her living with a man who evoked such deep negative emotions in an otherwise even-tempered person like Stacy. "But you still want children?"

"I do. I've grown to see my students as my babies, and in my heart, they always will be. But I still want a child I can call mine. I've thought about adoption, but the process is too arduous, and the likelihood of a single black mother adopting a baby—that isn't on withdrawal from something—is next to zero. IVF is expensive. I'm hoping God will bless me with the right man to come along and help me accomplish that dream."

He kissed her hand again. "Maybe He already has."

TWENTY-TWO

Cooper stood in the doorway with flowers and a bottle of sparkling wine. He leaned in and gave Stacy a kiss. "Mmmm… I've been looking forward to that all day."

"So have I," she replied. "Best part of my day—so far." He arched an eyebrow and she laughed. "I'm talking about dinner and our movie."

"Oh." He made a face, making Stacy laugh harder. "Smells good. What can I do?"

"How about the salad? I have everything out on the on the counter."

"One salad coming up." He hung up his coat then followed her into the kitchen. He washed his hands and began assessing the ingredients.

"Alexa, play my cooking mix," Stacy said. The device responded affirmatively, then began playing a funky upbeat tune with a slight Caribbean beat. Cooper listened as a man's voice came through, but he was mesmerized by Stacy. As the music played, she swayed back and forth. Even her moves on top of the stove were rhythmic to the music. With every beat, Cooper felt himself drawn to her svelte curves. An unfamiliar longing grew inside. He'd been attracted to women before, and he knew when he was being seduced. This was different. He knew she wasn't trying to seduce him. Her moves were instinctual, natural. Everything she did was exquisite. She just connected with him in a way no one else ever had.

"You doing okay over there," she asked, breaking his thoughts.

"Oh…uh, yeah. I could use some water." *And a cold shower.* She brought him a glass of ice water, which he gulped down. "I had an idea."

"Yeah?" She moved in closer. "Is this what you had in mind?" She put her hands around his face and pulled him in for a kiss, soft at first, then quickly gaining in intensity. Just as quick as she started, she ended it abruptly. She pulled back and smiled. "You were saying?"

"Lord…," he muttered. "I could use more water." She pointed him to her refrigerator, and he refilled his glass. *Good Lord, that woman knows how to kiss.* "This idea I had—not that yours wasn't impressive—but I was thinking, I'd like to throw you a party."

"Why? It's not my birthday."

"It's not for you, exactly. It's to introduce you to some people who might want to invest in CCA."

She stopped mashing the potatoes to face him. "Are you serious?"

"I am. I know a lot of people who like investing in the arts and in youth organizations. CCA sits right in that intersection. I think we can get some serious donations to get an endowment started. You could offer free to low-cost classes to the community and provide even more scholarships."

"That sounds amazing, Cooper. Thank you." She turned back to the potatoes, blinking back tears. *God, this man is too good to be true. Did you really send him to me to help my dreams come true?* She glanced over her shoulder and watched as he prepared the salad. *How does he look even sexier slicing cucumbers?*

❧ ☙

As the end credits of the original *West Side Story* rolled, Stacy turned to Cooper and asked, "Well, what did you think?"

He shrugged. "Musicals aren't my thing, but this one was pretty good. I see why Rita Moreno got the Oscar."

Stacy nodded. "She was so amazing. Her heartbreak, her rage, her joy. She gave it all. I still think Natalie Wood was miscast, but that last scene when Tony died, you really felt her heart breaking."

"I agree." Cooper stretched and yawned, then checked his watch. "I should get going. I've got an early call tomorrow." He leaned in and kissed her. "This was wonderful. Next movie night, *The Equalizer*."

"I'll watch anything with Denzel," she said, wiggling her eyebrows.

Cooper rolled his eyes. "I don't get women's obsession with that man."

"Don't be hatin' on Denzel or we may have to fight." She threw up her fists in a mock stance.

He held up his hands in surrender. "I give." They stood, then walked to the front door. Grabbing his coat, he said, "I have some extra tickets to the Alvin Ailey performance next month. Would you like to go?"

"Yes, of course! I'd love to go. I'd love to bring Mama and Toye. Maybe Eric could join us. How many extra tickets do you have?"

"About a hundred."

TWENTY-THREE

The coach bus pulled up in front of CCA's building. Cooper stepped off and walked to the entrance to find about sixty eager children and teens along with their happy parents waiting. "Alright everyone, let's load up," he called, pointing to the direction of the bus. Many of the children cheered seeing the large charter bus. He could see them scrambling to find seats while marveling at the size and comfort of the vehicle. Many parents thanked him for setting up the trip, which he humbly accepted.

Rose and Stacy were the last ones to board after they locked up the facility. As her mother took her seat, Stacy asked the bus driver to show her how to speak over the PA system. "Ladies and gentlemen." She paused as everyone settled in and gave her their full attention. "Is everyone excited for our outing today?" The cheers and applause resounded throughout the bus. "Before we depart, let's take a moment to thank the MBIY Foundation and our benefactor, Mr. Cooper Banks, for this opportunity." Cooper stood and waved as a chorus of thank-yous echoed. "Let's have a quick prayer. Father, thank you for this opportunity. Thank You for the foundation, for Cooper, and our driver. We ask that You bless us as we travel and return us home in safety and in peace. In Jesus' name, amen."

Stacy took her seat in the aisle across from her mother and next to Cooper. "It's a shame Toye couldn't come," Rose said.

"She's going to meet us at the theater, Mama," Stacy replied. "She claimed she had some work to do this morning, but I know she didn't want to ride the bus with a bunch of excitable children."

"Not the kid-friendly type," Cooper said.

"She loves kids. She's the best aunt. She spoils her nieces and nephews rotten. But then she can send them home," she said, snickering.

Cooper noticed the red wool coat Rose was wearing. "That's a beautiful coat, Mama Rose."

"Thank you, Cooper," she said. "Stacy bought it for me last Christmas. My favorite color," she added, stroking the arm.

"It looks good on you."

Rose blushed and Stacy pinched him on his leg. "Are you trying to score points with my mother," she whispered.

"Only if it scores points with you," he said, kissing her on the cheek. "I have a surprise for you."

"What is it?"

"You'll have to wait until after the show."

❧ ❧

As the dancers took their final bows, the audience gave them a rousing standing ovation. The rest of the audience members began departing the theater, but Cooper indicated that their group should remain seated. A tall, dark-haired woman made her way over to where Cooper was standing. "Mr. Banks? Is this your group?"

"Yes, it is. And this is Stacy Roberts, the executive director of Chi City Arts," he said.

The woman extended her hand. "It's very nice to meet you. I'm Violet Jacobs, director of community relations here at the Auditorium Theater. When Mr. Banks contacted us, he thought your group might like to take a tour backstage and meet some of the dancers."

Stacy shook her head as a grin split her face. "That would be amazing, thank you!" She gestured for Violet to follow her, and they took a spot in front of the group. "Hey everyone, this is Ms. Violet Jacobs, and she has a surprise for us."

Violet nodded and grinned. "I'm so excited that you all came here today. Did you enjoy the show?" She laughed as everyone responded enthusiastically. "Show of hands, how many of you have never been the Auditorium Theater before?" Hands shot up everywhere. "That's terrific. Here at the theater, when we have first-time guests, we like to give them something special."

"A t-shirt?" one kid asked.

"A poster?" another asked.

"Yes, but today, we're going to do something different," Violet said. "How would you like to take a tour backstage and meet some of the dancers you just saw on stage?" She reared back as the group screamed and jumped up and down in excitement. "Why don't you leave your coats here and line up and follow me? Moms and dads, please join us. We will have security to watch your belongings."

As the group lined up, Stacy said, "Let's remember we are young professionals, and this is a professional space. If you have questions, raise your hand and don't touch anything that isn't touching you." Violet took the lead and began the tour with a brief history of the theater.

Stacy hung back at the rear with Cooper. "Is this the surprise?"

"One of them," he replied, grinning.

The tour ended up with everyone on the stage. Violet showed them the orchestra pit and explained some performances in the theater were done with musicians playing the score live, unlike the dance performance, which used prerecorded tracks. They were about to head to their seats when the executive director of the dance company came out to greet them. "It's so nice to meet young dancers," he said. "How many of you would like to dance on this stage one day?" Hands shot up and a chorus of "me" seemed to tickle him. "How about now?"

"What?" Stacy said.

"How about right now?"

Stacy fumbled for words as the kids crowded around her begging her to let them dance. "It's a nice offer, but we're not prepared to dance today."

"How about the finale you did at the gala?" Cooper said. "That was terrific."

"We don't have our music, Cooper."

"I took care of that. Go on. Let them dance," he whispered.

"Please?" Arianna begged. "This is the chance of a lifetime."

"Are you sure, kids? None of you are dressed properly, and we haven't practiced that number since last fall."

"I remember," Kenzie piped up.

"We can do this," Arianna said. She began unlacing her boots and stepping out in her sock feet. The other kids followed suit.

Stacy shrugged, shaking her head in amazement. "Okay. Let's get into positions. If you have on ballet flats, keep them on. The rest of you, watch your step." Everyone who wasn't part of the dance team made their way back to their seats, whipping out their phones to record as Stacy mentally reworked the positions to accommodate the much larger stage.

"Hang on," the director said. He went to Violet and whispered to her, and she exited the stage. Minutes later, she returned with the dance company following her. The kids gasped. "We're gonna dance in front of the Alvin Ailey company? We're not ready," Arianna exclaimed.

"You wanted to do this," Stacy said. She took a breath, then gathered the kids in. "They're people, just like us. And yes, they're professional dancers, but they were once kids just like you. So just do your best, understood?"

"Heard," the children responded. She guided them through a couple of deep breaths to help settle their nerves, then repositioned them. Taking a deep breath herself, she turned to the center stage. "Thank you so much for this opportunity. Ladies and gentlemen, it is my honor to present the dance company of Chi City Arts." She exited to the side of the stage and nodded to the director. He raised his hand, signaling the audio tech to begin playing the music. As soon as it came on, the kids went right into their routine.

Stacy watched, mesmerized. She knew this routine inside and out. Tears rolled down her face as remembered her own time on a stage very much like this one and the dreams that went unfulfilled. She was thrilled for her students. She knew many of them would never have a chance like this again. She also knew there was a possibility that one or two of them would be joining a company like Alvin Ailey's soon.

Cooper came behind her and wrapped his arms around her. "Thank you for this," she said, her voice thick with emotion. "You don't know what this means."

He nodded. "I'm beginning to understand."

The kids hit their final pose as the music ended and the assembled audience of dancers and families rose to their feet in a standing ovation. She wiped her face and smiled as the children excitedly ran over to where she and Cooper were standing, and she greeted them with open arms. "You were amazing. I am so very proud of you."

Arianna clutched her chest. "Ohmigosh! I am never going to forget this day. I *am* going to be on that stage again," she declared.

Stacy cupped her cheek fondly. "I know you will, sweetheart. You're on your way."

The director came up to Stacy. "Excellent work, young people. You should be very proud." He extended his hand to Stacy. "What a tremendous job you've done with your students. I see great potential in many of them."

"I appreciate the compliment," Stacy replied, "but the credit goes to them. They work hard."

"Yes, but you've taught them well." He looked around at the children. "How would you like a chance to dance with our company?" He grinned as the children eagerly jumped up and down. "Do you have time? It'll only be about 30 minutes or so."

Stacy looked at Cooper, who nodded. "We have the bus all day. I'll push back our dinner reservation." He grabbed his phone and left the stage before Stacy could question him.

The director called up some of his dancers and had them section the children in groups. "Ms. Roberts, why don't you join us," the director asked.

Stacy nodded, fighting back fresh tears that threatened to brim over again. She joined a couple of the pro dancers in their own group, quickly picking up the intense choreography. She kept an eye on her students, pleased that they were learning new techniques and steps, some beyond their capabilities, but they did their best to keep up. She could see the joy in Arianna's eyes as she listened and learned her choreography.

Finally, the director called everyone together. He explained they were going to perform a group dance on stage. Each group was being led by a professional dancer with the children following along when it was their group's turn. The dance captain of Stacy's group whispered, "We're the last group. We want you to take the lead."

Stacy's eyes grew large. "Are you sure?"

"You've got this," the woman said. "Trust me. Besides, your students will get a kick out of seeing you dance."

Stacy nodded. *Breathe, girl. Focus on the steps.* It's the same advice she'd given her students before every performance. *It's no big deal. They've seen you dance before.* "Not like this," she whispered to herself.

The director asked the parents to get in position to record the performance. Once everyone was in place on stage, he cued the music. She was delighted to see how well her kids were doing. Kenzie's confidence level seemed to grow exponentially as she completed her moves. When Arianna's group took their turn, Stacy nodded appreciatively. The teen was side by side with the veteran dancer, and it was clear she was headed for a career on the stage.

"We're up next," the dance captain said. Stacy refocused and waited for her cue as the captain counted down. "Five, six, seven, eight."

Stacy took off, twisting, turning, leaping across the stage. Even though the choreography was new, it felt like she had been performing it for years. It took seconds to realize that the rest of her group, made up of the professionals, was standing to the side, allowing her to have the spotlight. For this moment in time, she didn't care. She was on a professional stage, living her dream. Nothing mattered in the moment: not her past, not her present, not her future, not Vincent, not Cooper, not her mother. The only thing that mattered to Stacy was the dance.

It seemed like an eternity, but it was over in minutes. She was brought back to reality by the screams of her students, most of whom were in awe of their teacher.

"You were so beautiful!"

"I didn't know you could dance like that!"

"Amazing!"

"Ms. Stacy, that was fire," Arianna called out.

Stacy's group of dancers came running over and gave her hugs. "Thank you for this moment," Stacy said.

"You deserved it," the dance captain said. "You belong on this stage."

"I wholeheartedly agree," the director said, coming up to shake her hand. "I know this program is yours, but if you ever want another chance to dance professionally, I know people who would love to have you as a part of their company. Let's stay in touch." He handed her a card. Clapping his hands, he said, “Great job everyone! Let’s get together downstage and take some pictures.”

Once the last picture was taken, the children scrambled to get themselves together. They begged to see the videos and pictures. Stacy took a few moments to steady herself before approaching the parents, who were falling all over themselves thanking her for the opportunity and alternately complimenting her on her performance. “I had no idea any of this was going to happen. We can thank…” She looked around and saw Cooper in the aisle talking with Violet. “Everyone, let’s thank Mr. Banks and Ms. Jacobs for a fantastic experience.” Everyone burst into applause and cheers.

Mama Rose walked up to her daughter, the tears still running down her face. “I’m so proud of you, baby. You were born for the stage.”

Stacy shrugged. “It just wasn’t meant to be.” She turned to Cooper. “You set all this up, didn’t you?”

He held out his hands. “Surprise.”

“This—” she waved her arms around, “this is too much. The tickets were more than enough, but the tour? The opportunity to perform on stage—here? The mini-dance class?”

Shrugging, he said, “I told you, I know people. The foundation is a major donor to Alvin Ailey. I met Violet at another charity function. We stayed in touch. I made a personal donation to the theater, and she agreed to set everything up.” Turning his attention to the group, he clapped his hands and called out, “Hey, who’s hungry?”

❧ ☙

The excitement from their theater experience had not diminished as the CCA group chowed down on pizza at Giordano's. They gorged on all manner of thin and deep-dish pizzas and desserts. By the time they loaded the bus and pulled off, many of the children and their parents had drifted off to sleep. A few parents held low-key conversations, sharing videos and photos with each other.

Rose had also nodded off by one of the window seats. Stacy sat next to Cooper with her head on his shoulder, a soft smile on her face. He rubbed his thumb over the back of her hand in a gentle caress. She'd already thanked him profusely for the afternoon's surprises. Stacy finally found herself calming down from the high that she'd been on since their earlier excursion.

"Ms. Stacy?" Arianna stood in the aisle. She noticed the couple's closeness. "Oh, my bad. I'll talk to you later."

Stacy sat up. "No, it's fine, Arianna. Sit down, please. What's up?"

The girl sat in the seat next to Rose, clutching her phone in her hands. "Remember how we had a chance to talk to the dancers on stage?"

"Of course."

"My dance captain, she really liked how I performed. She suggested I should take some classes with their company here in Chicago."

"I think that's a great idea, Arianna."

"But I don't want to leave CCA."

"You don't have to. I'm pretty sure they have classes that can work around your schedule. I think with your talent, you could earn a scholarship."

"Really? Because what she really suggested is that I apply for one of their summer intensives in New York. And if that goes well, I could maybe apply to be in their program at Fordham University. I made a deal with my mom that if I wanted to pursue dance, I still had to get my degree."

"Arianna, I agree with your mother. You have the talent to go far as a dancer, but having your degree gives you something to use once your dance career is over. You could become a choreographer, an instructor, or own your own studio one day, if that's your desire."

"Yeah," the teen said. "I get that. We just have to figure out how we can pay for it all. With my CCA scholarship, mom thinks we could maybe swing the classes here, but she doesn't see how we'll be able to afford New York. It's not just the classes, but we'd have to find a place to stay. Mom won't let me stay in New York by myself, but since her job lets her work remotely, she'd come with me." She sighed. "Not like it's going to happen anyway."

"Arianna," Cooper said, "Don't give up your dream just yet." He pulled out his phone. "I'm going to give you my phone number. Give me your mom's contact information. If you get accepted into the program, have your mother contact me and we'll work out the financials."

Tears sprang in the girl's eyes. "Are you serious?"

"Absolutely. What's her number?" They exchanged information and confirmed its receipt.

"Omigosh! Thank you, Mr. Banks! I gotta go tell mom!" Arianna leapt from her seat and raced to the back where her mother was sitting.

"Cooper, you didn't have to do that," Stacy said.

"Do what? I told you that the foundation donates to the Ailey company. If she's talented enough to get accepted, I'll make sure there's scholarship money. And my company has corporate apartments in New York. They could stay there rent-free. If they want to pay a small stipend, that's fine, too. It's no big deal. The apartment is only used when I'm in town. I don't mind staying at a hotel if I have business there next summer."

She leaned in and kissed him. "Have I told you today how amazing you are?"

"No. But I'll let you make it up to me with another kiss."

"Gladly."

TWENTY-FOUR

Stacy was sitting at a table in a café, downing two dulce de leches. Sitting across from her was Cooper, smirking. Their conversation was being drowned out by a Cuban band playing a familiar tune. A sultry dancer moved by their table. Cooper got up and began dancing with her. Not to be outdone, Stacy found her own partner and shimmied past Cooper and his partner. Cooper grabbed Stacy and began dancing with her. The other woman grabbed Stacy and shoved her out the way. Stacy hauled off and slugged her. A fight broke out among the café patrons, but Cooper flung Stacy over his shoulder and made their way to a courtyard.

"I can hear bells ringing," she said. "Ding, dong, ding, dong."

"Answer them," Cooper replied.

"I don't want to," she said.

"Mama is calling," he said, in a voice that sounded suspiciously like Siri.

Stacy groaned as she opened her eyes. Peeking at the clock, she could hear her phone announcing her mother was indeed calling her. She groaned, then picked up the phone. "Ma, it's my one day off this month. I told you I was sleeping in. Why in God's name are you calling me at seven-thirty in the morning?"

"I know, baby, and I'm sorry," Rose said. The glee was evident in her voice. "But you won't believe what's happened!"

"Did you win the lottery finally? And if you did, couldn't you have called me later?"

"It's not that good, but almost!"

"Mama, what is going on?"

"I got a new car!"

Stacy shot up in bed. "What did you say?"

"Baby, I got up and opened the curtains and there it was, sitting in front of the house with a big red bow on it! Oh, hallelujah!"

"Ma, can you please stop? Where did it come from?"

"The Lord, baby, the Lord!"

Hardly. "Can you calm down long enough and send me a picture?"

"I already did! Oooh baby, I cannot wait to take this for a drive!"

Stacy shook her head as her mother continued her celebration. Her phone chimed with a new message. As she was going to check the photo, another call came in. "Mom, I'll call you back. Toye's on the other line."

"Girl!" Toye screeched. "What the devil is happening?"

"Let me guess."

"Why did some random stranger ring my doorbell and hand me the keys to a brand-new car! And then ask me to open my garage so they could install the charging kit?"

Stacy rolled her eyes. "Cooper," she sighed.

"Cooper! Why would he buy me an electric car?"

"Because I never learned the difference when someone is playing games and when they're playing me."

"What?"

"Never mind." The doorbell rang and Stacy knew what was behind it. "Gotta run. Cooper's here."

"You don't sound too thrilled," Toye said.

"I'm not. I'll call you later." She disconnected the call, grabbed her robe, then ran downstairs to answer the door. She snatched it open to find a grinning Cooper standing there with keys in his hand. Behind him, she noticed a new Aviator with a bright red bow on top, just like in the stupid Christmastime commercials she hated.

"Surprise!" he said. "These belong to you."

Instead of taking the keys, she grabbed him by the jacket and pulled him inside. "Cooper, what the hell?" she hissed.

His grin faded. "Excuse me?"

"What do you think you're doing? First Mama, then Toye, now me? You think you can buy our affections?"

"Hold on," he said holding out his hands. "Why are you so angry? I thought you'd be thrilled."

"Try furious. I didn't ask you to buy cars for anyone, especially not me."

"I didn't say you did. You need a car and so does your mom. Toye was just a bonus. I wanted to do this for you. By the way, I bought the sprinter trucks for CCA."

"Nobody asked you to!"

"You said you needed them."

"It was a game, Cooper, remember? We were pretending! That was not an open invitation for you to swoop in with all your money playing fairy godfather."

"I wasn't trying to—"

"Get out."

"What?"

"I said get out," Stacy said. She walked over to the door and held it open. "Please leave."

Cooper laid the keys on the coffee table. Shaking his head, he said, "I won't apologize for doing something nice for you. And I won't apologize for the purchases I made for CCA. The car is yours. Do whatever you want with it."

Once he was gone, she closed the door, slid to the floor and began to cry.

❧ ❧

"Cooper Banks, get in here," Mama Rose said, wrapping him in a hug. "You have outdone yourself." She pulled back and saw the stricken look on his face. "What's wrong?"

He shook his head. "I just left your daughter's house. I bought her a car, too, but she was furious. She accused me of trying to buy her affections, then she threw me out."

"That's not like her," Rose said. "Come on in tell me everything." She led him into her living room. He sat on the couch. "Would you like a cup of coffee? I know it's after breakfast, but I have some biscuits and sausage in the kitchen if you're hungry."

"No, thanks anyway." He waited until she took a seat in the recliner. "What did I do wrong?"

Rose folded her hands. "First, tell me why you bought the cars."

He frowned. "Why wouldn't I?"

"That's not an answer."

He leaned back. "I knew she needed a car. And when we went to the auto show she mentioned that CCA needed the vans."

Rose nodded. "You bought vans—plural?"

"I did. It's no big deal. It's an investment in CCA. I can write them off," he answered, shrugging.

"I understand that. But why did you buy a car for me? And not just any old car, but a top of the line, fully loaded Benz, customized exactly like I would have picked for myself?"

He hung his head and chuckled. "I wanted to do something nice for you and for Toye."

"You bought Toye a car too?"

"I did."

"Did Stacy ask you to do this?"

He shook his head. "We were talking at the auto show. We were playing a game and I asked her to imagine if she could buy anything she wanted, what would she do. She told me what she'd do for you and for Toye and for herself."

"So, you took it upon yourself to do this.

"Yes."

"And you expected her to be grateful."

"Yes."

"And you lied to her."

Cooper paused. "I didn't lie to her."

Rose cocked her head to one side. "But you didn't tell her what you were planning. You asked her to imagine something, then you went and did it without telling her what you were planning."

"It was supposed to be a surprise."

Rose gave him a wan smile. "Tell me again, Cooper. Why did you buy all these vehicles?"

He sighed. "Stacy is important to me. And I know how much you and Toye mean to her. I wanted to do something nice for the people who mean the most to her."

"That's very sweet, Cooper," Rose said, shaking her head. "It's not what you did; it's how you went about it."

"I don't understand."

"She told you about her first husband, didn't she?"

"She did. The things he did…"

"Yes. He was a horrible man. We didn't know it at first. He was kind and charismatic. He had money and he wasn't afraid to throw it around to get what he wanted. But he also used his money to manipulate Stacy. He used it to maintain his power and control over her. When he finally decided she was of no value to him, he left her with nothing. He took every dime she had made and kept it from her. If not for her lawyer, she would have been destitute, sacked with medical bills that would have kept her in debt for years.

"You played her, Cooper. You knew what you were planning, but she didn't. You saw a need and you thought you were doing something nice. The way she sees it, you lied to her, and you were using your money to manipulate not just her, but Toye and me as well, so that we would accept you and encourage Stacy to be with you."

"That's not what I was trying to do," Cooper said.

"Maybe, but she's been burned before. So have I. We won't get fooled again, Cooper. I won't allow it." She leaned forward. "I asked you once before what your intentions were with my daughter. I've been praying about you and Stacy. And I know what the Lord has told me, but I need to hear it from you."

Cooper leaned forward and took the older woman's hands in his. "I care a great deal for Stacy. I believe in my heart that she is the one for me. I would never do anything to hurt her, or you. I want nothing but good things for you both. I want her to have everything her heart desires. And if I can get her to forgive me, I'll do whatever it takes to make this up to her."

Rose's smile was warm and genuine. "I believe you, son."

"I apologize, Mama Rose, if this made you uncomfortable in any way. I'll take the car back if you want."

"Are you kidding? I'm not offended in the slightest. I love my new ride."

TWENTY-FIVE

Frustrated by the morning's events, Stacy did what she always did when she was out of sorts—dance. Up in her studio, she tapped on a music playlist of instrumental jazz and gospel. She stretched and began a freestyle dance infused with ballet, jazz, and hip hop. When the music changed, so did her dance. Her dance was interrupted by her ringing cell phone. Taking a moment to catch her breath, she greeted her mother. "Hi Mama."

"Hi baby. Working out?"

"Something like that. What's up?"

"I spoke with Cooper."

Stacy rolled her eyes. Grabbing a towel to dry off, she said, "Did you fall all over yourself thanking him for the new ride?"

"You're out of line, young lady," Rose scolded.

"I'm sorry, Mother."

"I sat him down and had a nice conversation with him. I believe he meant no harm."

"He lied to me."

"And he knows he was wrong for that. I know it seems like he's doing the same thing as Vincent, but I promise, he's nothing like that man. You have to trust me on this one. You must trust God on this one."

"I don't know…"

"He's on his way over to talk to you. Listen to him, not just with your ears, but with your heart."

The doorbell rang. "He's here."

"What are you going to do?"

"What choice do I have? I'll call you later." She wrapped the towel around her neck and headed downstairs to the door. Cooper stood on the other side, holding a bouquet of blue hyacinths.

"I'd like to apologize. Will you hear me out?" he asked.

She shrugged. "Come in." She accepted the flowers and took them to the kitchen to put them in a vase with some water. "Would you like something to drink?" He shook his head. She grabbed a glass of water then took a seat opposite him. "You spoke with Mama."

"I did," he said. "She set me straight. I am so sorry. I honestly thought that I was doing something nice for you and your mom and Toye. I see now that I lied to you when I said we were pretending. I should have told you what I was thinking, and I should have asked if you were okay with that."

"Yes, you should have. Cooper, I don't need you or your money to rescue or do for me and mine. We were fine before you came into our lives, and we'll be fine if you walk out. What I don't want is for you to use your money to do things because you think it will impress me."

"That's not what I was trying to do."

"Are you sure about that? I mean, the Alvin Ailey tickets, the backstage passes, the impromptu class, Arianna's scholarship, you're telling me you didn't do any of that to ingratiate yourself with me?"

He paused to gather his thoughts. "If I'm being honest, yes, part of me was trying to impress you. But I really did want the kids to enjoy the show. The tour and the class were bonuses. As for Arianna, the offer is legitimate. I've seen her dance twice and to my untrained eye, she has potential. I just want her to have a chance to pursue her dreams as far as she can go. So many African American children can't pursue arts careers professionally because they're hindered by finances. I don't want Arianna to miss out on her chance."

Stacy nodded, swallowing past the lump in her throat. "I know how true that is. But Cooper, your money doesn't impress me. It never has. What impresses me is your generous spirit, your kind heart. You make me laugh. You watch musicals with me even though I know they irritate you on some level. I feel safe and secure with you, something I haven't felt in a very long time. When you throw your money around, I don't see the real Cooper. I see someone who uses money to control and manipulate others. I don't want to be with that person. I've already done that, and I won't go there again."

He reached over and took her hands in his. "I will never hurt you, Stacy. If you want me to promise to keep my money to myself, I will. If you want me to promise to discuss with you anything I want to do for you, I will. I just want to be a part of your life. I want you to know in your heart that I will protect you, support you, and cherish you now and always." He wiped a tear that rolled down her face. "Do you believe me?"

"I want to," she whispered. "It's hard."

"I know. I will do whatever you need me to do to prove to you that you can trust me. Will you give me that chance?" He pulled her hands to his lips and kissed them.

She closed her eyes. "Yes."

He leaned in and kissed her. “I’m glad. Now, do you want me to take back the truck? I will have it picked up. Just say the word.”

She smiled and shook her head. “No, I’ll keep it.”

“You sure?”

“I am. I know you meant well. And I’m sorry I threw you out earlier.”

“Forgiven.”

TWENTY-SIX

Spring made an early appearance in Chicago. The sun broke through the clouds making everything seem brighter, and bringing with it warmth that, after the cold winter, found its citizens taking to the streets, playing in the parks, gardening at their homes, and enjoying the sights and sounds of the city. It coincided with spring break, which was a welcome break for Stacy and her staff. With an open Saturday morning, she decided to hop in her new SUV and take it for a drive.

Her summer music medley was blaring through the speakers when her phone rang. Cooper's face popped up on the screen. "Hey handsome."

"What are you doing today," Cooper asked, his voice resounding through Stacy's Bluetooth speakers.

"I'm taking a drive down Lake Shore Drive with my sunroof open," she said, grinning.

"Sounds like fun. Where are you headed?"

"Nowhere in particular. Why?"

"Want to head down to Navy Pier?"

"I'll pick you up."

❧ ❧

They took an afternoon lunch cruise around the lake, dancing and spending time on the top deck enjoying the sunshine. After debarking, they took turns on the carousel, the Wave Swinger and the Drop Tower.

Exiting the last ride, Stacy clutched Cooper's arm. "Why did I let you talk me into getting on that terrifying contraption?"

"You didn't enjoy it," he asked, wrapping his arm around her.

"You mean being sling shot into space and then falling back like a stone? No, I didn't."

"So that's why you were laughing so hard."

"Those were cries of terror."

"Yeah right. Ready to get something to eat?"

"I'd much rather get a drink," Stacy said.

The walked along the boardwalk until they arrived at the Margaritaville Bar & Grille. The restaurant was crowded, but the hostess was able to seat them quickly. They ordered volcano nachos as an appetizer and drinks to go with them. As they waited for their food, Stacy asked, "Tell me something. If you couldn't be a billionaire-investment banker-philanthropist, what would you be?"

He took a sip of his water. "A veterinarian."

"Seriously?"

"Yes. I love animals."

"But you don't have any pets."

"True, and I don't want any, but I think I'd have made a good animal doctor."

"Really?"

"No, I'm kidding." He took a punch in the arm from her. "Ow. You hit like a girl." He laughed as she fake swung again.

"Seriously," she said, "what would you have done?"

"I don't know. I wasn't much of an athlete. I think I would have become a high school math teacher."

That surprised her. "Why?"

He shrugged. "My family has always been about helping others. I love math. I spent a lot of time tutoring my classmates, starting in elementary school. I think teaching would have been a natural choice for me."

"I could see that." The appetizers arrived and Cooper blessed the food.

"What about you," he asked. "If you weren't able to dance, what would you do?" At her cross look, he added, "Okay, bad choice of words. If you were able to choose another career besides dancing, what would you have chosen?"

"That's easy. Chemical engineering," she replied, popping a nacho in her mouth.

"Seriously?"

She laughed. "I barely passed chemistry in high school. No, I think if I had to choose any career besides dance or the arts, I would have been a lawyer, probably specializing in family law. I'd represent women and men in toxic relationships and make sure they were able to get custody of their children, that sort of thing."

From the look on her face, he surmised she was thinking of her ex-husband. Cooper changed the subject. "I learned this game in college where you give two options and have a person pick."

"And the winner gets a new car?"

"Ha-ha. No, it's a way to get to know another person. For instance, I say, *Godfather* or *Goodfellas*."

"*Godfather*," she replied.

"Cool. If you chose *Goodfellas*, I'd have to stop speaking to you," he said, chuckling. "Now you pick two."

She thought for a moment. "Michael Jordan or LeBron James."

He sat back in his chair. "You don't play, do you?"

"Answer, please."

"Jordan. All day. Baryshnikov or Gregory Hines?" he replied.

"From *White Nights*? Not fair. Baryshnikov."

"That's surprising," he said.

"I love Gregory Hines," Stacy said, "but when Baryshnikov did those twelve pirouettes, that was amazing."

"Fair enough. Your turn," he said.

"Let's try something simpler: lemonade or iced tea?"

"Both. Burger King or McDonald's?"

She made a face. "Neither. Aretha Franklin or Whitney Houston?"

"The Queen of Soul. Big Luther or little Luther?"

"That's not funny," she said, hiding a grin. "Okay, big Luther. Michael Jackson or Prince?"

"Michael. Hee-hee," he crowed.

"Don't ever do that again," she said, laughing.

The rest of the meal was spent talking about everything from movies to politics. They found more in common than not, but even their disagreements dissolved into laughter. When the check came, Cooper paid. "I'm stuffed. Feel like taking a walk?"

"Yeah, that would be nice."

They exited the restaurant for the boardwalk. The air had cooled, and Stacy shivered from the change in temperature.

Cooper took off his jacket and draped it around her shoulders. "Thanks, but aren't you cold?"

"Guess I'll have to keep you close to stay warm," he replied, wrapping his arm around her and pulling her close. "You feel like a ride on the Centennial Wheel?"

She grimaced. "I don't know. After that slingshot ride, I don't know how I feel about heights."

"This is so much different. It's slow and easy, I promise."

"Alright, let's do it."

They walked over to the line and waited for their turn to board one of the gondolas. Cooper eased up to the operator, whispered something in his ear, then shook the man's hand. When it was their turn to board, the ride operator let them on their gondola, then closed the door to other riders.

As promised, the ride moved smoothly upward. "What did you say to that man?"

"I asked if we could have a private ride. I wanted to enjoy this moment alone with you." He leaned back in the seat and sighed. "I live near the lake. The view when the sun sets over the city never gets old."

"It is spectacular," she agreed. "Have you flown into the city at night?"

"Yes, of course."

"I love the view. The city skyline all lit up, it's magical." As they ascended higher, she began taking pictures with her phone, including a couple of selfies with Cooper. "I'll have to bring Mama here one day. I think she'll really enjoy it. Maybe I'll FaceTime her."

"Wait," Cooper said. "There's something I've been meaning to say to you."

The serious look on his face gave her pause. "What's wrong?"

"Nothing. Nothing's wrong." He took the phone out of her hands and placed it on the seat next to him. "I've been waiting to tell you something, but I wanted to be sure before I said it, and I wanted to wait until the right moment. Being here with you, right now, right here, there's no better moment to tell you that I love you."

She gasped. "What?"

"I said I love you. I'm in love with you. I have been for a while now. I know it seems soon, and I know I've made some mistakes, and I'll probably make more, but I want you to know that if you'll give me the chance, I'll love you for the rest of your life."

"How," she whispered. "Why?"

"From the moment we met at the gala, you took my breath away. I didn't understand how quickly you got under my skin, but I couldn't shake you. I made that ridiculous bid for your time, because I wanted to be close to you. I wanted to learn who you are, why you are. The more I learned about you, the more I began to love you. I know you've been hurt before, so I wanted to go slow, and I'm okay if you don't feel the same way right now. I just wanted, needed you to know how I felt, and to see if there's a chance you might feel the same."

The tears shone in her eyes. Stacy ducked her head and tried to speak past the lump in her throat. He put his finger under her chin and lifted her face towards his. He wiped the tears that fell and said, "You don't have to say anything."

"I want to," she whispered. "I… I've been so afraid, Cooper. My last marriage did more than just bring an end to my career. It shattered my self-confidence in a way that I thought could never be repaired. When it came to love, I never allowed myself to grow close to any man, and I told myself I'd never trust another man with my heart. I never wanted to let another man have that kind of control over me. And I was fine with that, until I met you." She stroked his face. "I don't know when or how, but you broke down all my defenses. You've shown me what a good man is. I've been fighting it, but I can't fight anymore."

"Do you believe that I love you," he asked, kissing her lips.

"Yes."

"Do you believe I won't hurt you," he asked, kissing her again.

"Yes."

"Do you love me?"

Instead of responding, she leaned in for a kiss. When they parted, she said, "Yes, I love you, Cooper." She burst into tears, collapsing in Cooper's arms. He held her close, stroking her hair, kissing her head.

Tears subsiding, she said, "I'm sorry."

"For what?"

"I don't know why I'm crying. I guess I never expected to hear or say those words again, much less believe them."

"Would it help if I said it again?"

"Yes, please."

"I love you, Stacy Roberts."

"I love you, Cooper Banks."

TWENTY-SEVEN

After dropping Cooper off at his building with a long kiss goodnight, she put in a call to her best friend.

"Hey, girlfriend. What's going on?"

"Cooper told me he loved me."

Toye's squeal pierced through the speakers, making Stacy adjust the volume in the car. "Tell me everything."

"Not over the phone. I'm on my way to you."

Fifteen minutes later, Stacy pulled up to Toye's brownstone in Hyde Park. Toye was standing in the doorway holding two glasses of wine. "Get in here and talk. Spare me no details."

They went to the couch and Stacy spent the next few minutes recounting the day's events, from his spontaneous invite to the Pier, their lunch conversation, and the ride on the Centennial Wheel. Stacy jumped up from the couch and started pacing in the living room. "What on earth possessed me to tell him I love him?"

"Maybe because you love him?" Toye countered.

"I can't be in love with him."

"Why not?"

"Because. Because it's too soon! It's only been a couple of months. What do I really know about him?"

"You know he's kind, considerate, funny, compassionate, thoughtful, generous, and he's wild about you. Plus, he's fine and rich, which is just whipped cream and the cherry on top of the sundae."

"Vincent was fine and rich," Stacy said.

"Vincent was rich, but there was nothing fine about him. He was a monster who used and abused you to get what he wanted. Vincent was a sadistic bastard who got off on the power he held over you. Cooper is nothing like that."

Stacy stood still. "How do you know Cooper's not like that?"

Toye set down her wine glass. "From the first moment I met Vincent, I didn't like him. He was as phony as a three-dollar bill. Why do you think he kept trying to keep us apart? He knew if I could get you to see who he really was, you'd leave him, and he'd lose the best dancer he'd ever be lucky enough to work with." She stood and went over to her friend. "Cooper is nothing like Vincent. I know that it in my soul and in my spirit. If I thought for a moment that he was anything like your ex, I would have never let him get near you and certainly not invest in CCA. Cooper is a man of his word, Stacy. If he says he loves you, I believe it. Do you?"

Stacy shrugged. "I want to."

"What does the Spirit say?"

She wiped a tear. "That I should trust that he loves me."

"There's your answer, girlfriend."

"I don't want to be wrong again," Stacy whispered.

Toye hugged her friend. "Not this time. This time, you hit the jackpot."

ĉ§ ĉ§

"I told Stacy I loved her." Cooper looked at his best friend to gauge his reaction.

Eric leaned against the counter, drinking from a bottle of water. "Took you long enough."

"You knew?"

"I'm your best friend. I could see it the first time you met."

"She thought *we* were a couple."

Eric spit out his water. "That's hilarious!"

"She hated me."

"She hated your game," Eric said, "which was weak, by the way."

"Whatever."

"What did she say? Don't tell me she put you in the friend zone."

"She said she loves me."

"That's great!" Eric clapped his hand on his friend's back. "I'm happy for you." Noting his friend's melancholy mood, he asked, "What's with that look? I thought you'd be jumping all over your couch."

Cooper sighed. "I'm not sure I believe her."

"Why not?"

"I don't know if she said it because I did, or because of the moment."

"How about she said because she meant it," Eric countered.

"How do I know for sure? I mean, we had a nice day together. Sitting at the top of the Centennial Wheel, overlooking the skyline, how could she not say it? Did I manipulate her into saying what I wanted to hear?"

Eric shook his head. "From what I know about her, she isn't afraid to tell you the truth, no matter if it hurts your feelings." He cocked his head. "What's the real reason you doubt her feelings for you?"

Cooper mulled over how much he should say to his friend. What Stacy had revealed about her first marriage was heartbreaking. The fact that she felt comfortable enough to tell him about it was huge for her. He didn't want to betray her trust, but he trusted his friend to keep his counsel. "She was married before. From what I know, he was rich, and he was mean. It was brief, and he did a lot of damage. Trusting any man with her heart—especially one who has money—isn't easy for her. Then I come along, using my money to get next to her."

"Yeah man, I get that. But you've shown her that you're different, that you only have her best interests at heart. That must count for something. Plus, unlike most of the clout-chasers you've dated in the past, she's interested in you, not your money. That's a miracle in itself," Eric said, laughing. "She's the real deal."

"I know. I don't know how or why it happened, but I know I can't imagine my life without her in it."

"Have you prayed about this?"

Cooper nodded. "Yeah, I've been praying for her since I met her."

"But have you prayed about your relationship with her? Have you prayed for her to be healed from her trauma? I'm a neurosurgeon. Fixing the physical issue is only half the battle. For a child to fully heal, they must overcome the mental and emotional trauma of their illness and surgery. Only then can they embrace their new life. From what you told me, the damage her ex did to her has to color how she feels about you and whether she can fully trust you and move forward."

Cooper paused. Had he been so infatuated with being with Stacy that he failed to see the damage her marriage had done to her? Did he not see all the roadblocks she'd thrown up because she wasn't sure she could trust herself, much less a man she'd only known for a sort time? He knew his feelings were real. If they were to have a future together, they'd have to get to the root of her trauma and deal with it, together. "I missed it. I fell head over heels for Stacy and I don't know if she's willing or able to move forward. I haven't brought this before the Lord."

"No time like the present," Eric said.

The men left the kitchen and went in the living room. Cooper knelt in front of his couch. Eric knelt beside him, resting his hand on Cooper's head.

"Father, we come to you tonight on behalf of my brother Cooper, and the woman of his heart, Stacy. You created us; You know all about us. You know all about Stacy and the hurt and anguish she went through. You know the scars around her heart. We pray that You will heal her heart fully and forever. We pray that You will guide Cooper as he walks with her, to be her helpmeet, her confidante, her forever-partner. Let Your love be reflected in their relationship. Help Cooper to love her the way Your word teaches us to love in 1 Corinthians 13: to be patient, kind, not jealous. Help Cooper not to seek his own motives, but to bear, believe, hope, and endure all things. We ask these things in the mighty and unfailing name of Jesus, amen."

TWENTY-EIGHT

The elevator in Cooper's building was empty, save for Stacy and Toye. Stacy checked her outfit one more time in the elevator's mirrored car. "Maybe I should have worn a dress instead of a pantsuit."

Toye rolled her eyes. "I told you, it's just a meet-and-greet, a glorified cocktail party. They're not interested in what you're wearing so much as what you have to say. Focus on making connections and telling CCA's story. That's what matters."

Stacy gripped her friend's hand. "I'm so glad you came with me."

"My pleasure. You know I've got your back."

"I know Eric will be happy to see you, too."

"He better be," Toye said, flicking her fresh braids over her shoulder. She made a quick turn. She smoothed down the skirt of her black wrap dress. "I'm worth it." She laughed and Stacy joined in.

The soft ping of the elevator indicated they were at the top floor of the building. The party room was around the corner, and they could hear the voices of the guests that had already arrived. "Are we late," Stacy asked.

"No. We're making an entrance. You're the guest of honor, remember?"

Cooper's assistant, Felicity, was waiting at the door. "Good evening, Stacy, Toye. You're right on time. If you'd like to hand off your wraps, you can come in and meet everyone. Cooper is already inside playing host."

They took off their wraps and handed them to a waiting coat check attendant. Stacy took a few steps, then stopped dead in her tracks. Sweat began to pool under her arms and her stomach roiled. Gripping Toye's arm, she asked Felicity, "Where's the restroom?"

Felicity saw her stricken expression and pointed to one near the kitchen area. "Right over there," she said.

Stacy ran to the restroom, with Toye following right behind. She barely made it to the toilet before she collapsed and began retching. Toye held Stacy's hair back as her body convulsed, emptying out everything she'd eaten all day. Towards the end, there was nothing left, and Stacy was wrapped in dry heaves. Toye applied cool paper towels to her friend's neck and forehead. Stacy rested against the wall, trying to will her breathing to slow down.

"Are you okay," Toye asked. "What happened?"

"He's here," she whispered.

"Who?"

"Vincent."

Toye's eyes grew large. "He can't be." She stood. "Wait here. I'll be right back."

"I'm not going anywhere."

Slowly opening the door, Toye pressed the lock button, then eased out of the bathroom and closed the door behind her. Felicity came rushing over. "Is everything alright? Is Stacy okay?"

"We'll see in a moment." Toye cut through the kitchen, Felicity trailing her, and made her way to the entrance of the party room. She scanned the guests until she saw him. He was talking with Cooper and Eric and a few other people. Fifteen years had passed since she'd last seen Vincent D'Ambrosio, but the only difference was the salt and pepper beard and the gray in his hair. If she didn't know better, she'd have sworn he was a distinguished professor or even a preacher. *A wolf in sheep's clothing is more like it.* Curiosity turned to fury in her face in a split second as Eric caught her eye. He beckoned for her to come but she turned back and nearly ran into Felicity.

"What the hell is he doing here?" she spat.

"Who?"

"That man talking to Cooper—Vincent D'Ambrosio. Did Cooper invite him?"

Felicity scanned the tablet she had in her hand. She shook her head. "No, he wasn't on the initial guest list. He came as a plus one with Cynthia Jackson, the woman in the green dress."

Eric came rushing up. "Hey, what's going on? Why didn't you come over?" He looked around. "Where's Stacy?"

"We're leaving," Toye said, ignoring Eric's questions. "Give Mr. Banks our regrets."

Eric took her hand. "Wait a minute, what happened?"

She snatched her hand from his. "He had me fooled. He played us all. I could kick myself for encouraging her to be with him." She turned on her heel and headed towards the bathroom.

Eric and Felicity followed, just as Toye coaxed Stacy out of the bathroom. Her eyes were red from vomiting and crying, but she managed to stand up on her own. "I have to get out of here," she said.

"Let's go." Toye wrapped a protective arm around her friend and guided her out towards the elevators. "You can have our wraps sent to Stacy's. Better yet, burn them," she said to Felicity.

"Toye, wait," Eric said. "Tell me what's going on. Let me get Cooper and we'll get this worked out."

"There's nothing to work out," Toye spat. "Your friend has terrible taste in friends." The elevator pinged and the women stepped on. "That includes you." The doors closed, leaving Eric standing there, confused.

&

Eric and Felicity rejoined Cooper and his guests in the party room. "Where'd you go? I thought I heard Toye. Is Stacy here?"

Vincent spoke up. "I was just asking our host when our guest of honor was arriving."

"Coop, I need to speak with you, privately. Please excuse us," Eric said. He tugged on his friend's arm and led him out towards the kitchen, with Felicity following closely.

"What's going on," Cooper asked.

"Toye and Stacy were here," Eric answered. "They just left."

"Why? What happened?"

"I'm not exactly sure, but I think it had something to do with that dude you were talking to in there, Vincent."

Felicity pulled out her tablet. "Vincent D'Ambrosio. He is Ms. Jackson's guest."

"I don't understand," Cooper said.

His assistant shifted on her feet. "Ms. Roberts was on her way inside. Suddenly, she asked where the bathroom was. I heard her throwing up. A few minutes later, Ms. Hawkins came out and she asked if Mr. D'Ambrosio was inside."

"Toye was pissed," Eric continued. "In so many words, she said we could both go jump."

"What about Stacy?" Cooper asked.

"She looked like she was ready to pass out. Something really spooked her."

"Or someone," Cooper said. "Felicity, I need you to do a deep dive on that Vincent guy. I need to go find Stacy."

"Who is this guy?" Eric asked.

"I think he's her ex-husband." Cooper shook his head. "Of all the people to show up tonight. When I get my hands on him..."

"Coop, I know what you're thinking, but you need to slow your roll. You can't go out there and pop off on that guy," Eric said.

"Why not?"

"There are more people out there, invited here by you. You brought them here to contribute to CCA. You need to stand in for Stacy. Tell them she fell ill."

"Which is isn't far from the truth," Felicity said.

"Whoever this dude is, you can't let on you know who he is. Focus on getting the word out about CCA."

"We have other guests due to arrive," Felicity said, "including members of the media. The last thing you want is to cause a scene to embarrass you, CCA, or the foundation." To make her point, several new guests had arrived. Felicity went over to greet them and led them to the party room.

"I know what you're thinking, Coop," Eric said. "You go back to your guests. I'll try to find out where Stacy is and make amends."

Cooper clapped his best friend's shoulder. "Thanks man."

"Don't thank me yet. You didn't see Toye's face."

❧

As soon as the party broke up, Cooper headed to the garage. Calls to Stacy's phone when straight to voicemail. Toye hung up on him. Finally, he called Mama Rose, who simply said, "She's here."

Thirty minutes later, he pulled up to Rose's home. He jumped out the SUV and ran up to the front door. He was about the ring the bell, but an angry Toye greeted him. "You've got some nerve showing your face here."

"I know what you must be thinking..."

"You have no idea what I'm thinking. If it wasn't for the Holy Ghost, I'd tell you."

Rose came up behind her and pulled her away from the door. "Go take her some ginger ale." She waited for Toye to leave before speaking. "You promised me you wouldn't hurt her."

"I didn't mean to, Mama Rose. Please believe me," he pleaded.

"How could you invite that man to a party for my daughter?"

"He was not invited. He came with a guest. I had no idea who he was. Stacy never told me his name. Once I found out, it was all I could do not to lay him out."

"But you didn't."

"I couldn't do it. I didn't want the negative publicity."

"For you."

"For her! For CCA. I had to make sure the focus was on CCA, not him."

"Are you sure, Cooper? Because right now, I don't know that I believe you." She stepped outside and pulled the door closed. "I haven't seen my daughter this gutted in years. All the work she's done to pull herself together and stand on her feet got undone in fifteen seconds. What's worse, she trusted you to protect her. *I* trusted you."

"Mama Rose," Cooper pleaded, "I meant what I said. I never meant to hurt her. I'm in love with her. I would never do anything to set her back. I want to help set her free."

"It's not your job to set her free, Cooper. Only Christ can truly set her free."

"I know, Mama Rose, but I want to help her. I want to be there for her. I want her to know she can count on me through anything."

"Oh Cooper." Rose caressed his cheek. "I know you mean well. Stacy does too."

"Can I see her? Please?"

"Not tonight, Cooper. Give her time."

TWENTY-NINE

Vincent D'Ambrosio was a man used to getting what he wanted. He learned at an early age that people could be persuaded to give him what he wanted by tapping into what they thought they needed. In school, his teachers were motivated to increase his grades or give him extra credit just by him spending extra time "helping" after school. As he grew taller and broader, his size became his primary asset. He became known as a "protector" of the weak, who in turn did everything from running errands, to doing his homework for him.

Women were drawn to him, feeling the need to be by the side of a strong, successful man. The only reason he focused on the arts, specifically dance, was to move in and be around beautiful women. Starting his own company allowed him to cherry pick dancers not only with talent, but who were willing to do anything to have a shot at a career.

A friend invited him to a dance recital and suggested Vincent might find some untapped talent among the dancers, especially a young sixteen-year-old who had a promising career in front of her. Intrigued, he went and was instantly mesmerized by the lithe young woman who took the stage as lead dancer. In his mind, Vincent saw her as the next Misty Copeland, and he intended to make sure her success was his success. He learned Anastasia was living with her mother and abusive, uncaring stepfather. He'd charmed Rose, who wanted nothing more than to give her daughter a chance at a life she herself had never lived. Anastasia was happy to have the affection of a father-figure that cared. She'd even swore she was in love with him.

It had been flattering at first, but as she grew older and her shape filled out more, the more he wanted her in his bed. Careful not to cross the line too early, he quietly romanced her. He proposed on her eighteenth birthday. A week later, he took her to City Hall for their wedding. After lunch with her mother, their honeymoon was in the presidential suite at the Swissotel. There, he plied her with wine and flowers and taken her virginity. She was so eager to please him, she did whatever he commanded until he wore her out. The next morning, he packed her up and brought him to his condo, then took her to rehearsal. He warned her not to tell anyone they were married, lest they became resentful and wouldn't perform up to expectations.

At home, he made sure she had everything she needed, but it was at his discretion. Eventually, he found her desire for him to be too needy and claustrophobic. He began seeing other women, coming home and taking from her what he felt he was owed. When she objected, he made sure she knew she was his, and he was in control. If she dared complain, if she embarrassed him at rehearsal by not performing properly, she knew what was coming.

Once Anastasia became injured and the doctors were convinced she would no longer be able to perform, he discarded her like a pair of old, ratty shoes. He had her stuff sent back to her mother's home and had her served with divorce papers the day she was released from the hospital. He knew she would never contest it, but Anastasia's shark for a lawyer managed to force him to pay her hospital bills in exchange for her silence and agreeing to have the court records sealed. It was worth it because he had found his next protégé. He had no desire to be mired in a messy, public divorce.

He hadn't given Anastasia another thought in the past fifteen years. His current benefactor, Cynthia Jackson, had shown him a video from a gala presentation she'd attended. He would have dismissed it outright until he saw her—Anastasia, or Stacy, as she was calling herself. She had matured and though she'd gained weight, it only added to her sexiness. However, the real charge he got was from one of the teenage dancers who had done a solo performance. He found out her name was Arianna Foster. Like most teens, she had a social media profile. He did some research. She was sixteen, had been dancing with CCA her entire life, but more important, she came from a single-parent home. From what he could determine, the father was not in the picture. She was perfect.

He parked outside CCA's tiny studio and waited until Arianna and her mother pulled up. Stepping out of his black Navigator, he walked over and pasted on his most charming smile. "Excuse me," he called out. He saw the mother move protectively in front of her daughter. "I'm sorry if I frightened you. My name is Vincent D'Ambrosio. I'm a former colleague of your director, Stacy Roberts."

The mother visibly relaxed, but still stood alert. "How may I help you?"

He reached in his jacket pocket and pulled out a business card. "I'm the executive director of D'Ambrosio Dance. We're based in New York, and we're an up-and-coming company of young, exceptionally talented dancers. I'm always on the lookout for new talent."

"So," Dawn Foster said.

"So, Ms. Foster, I've seen lots of videos of your daughter. Arianna, is it?" He extended his hand to the young woman. "You are phenomenal, young lady."

"Thank you," Arianna said, giggling.

"I think you'd fit right in with our company. In fact, I believe you could be principal dancer in less than two years."

Arianna's eyes grew large. "Are you serious?"

He nodded. "If you join our program now, we will work with you and get you started on your career."

Arianna jumped and grabbed her mother's arm. "Mom, did you hear that? I could be principal dancer in two years."

Dawn looked Vincent up and down. Everything about him was perfectly polished and slick. Too slick. "My daughter is going to finish high school and go to college. Or at the very least, she'll be joining a dance conservatory."

"Mom!"

Vincent chuckled. "You know I completely understand. Education is very important, and I agree. All my dancers have graduated from high school with honors."

"What about college?"

Vincent shrugged. "I think college has its place. They do a great job training dancers. I'm in the business of launching performance artists. Sure, you could go to college and take classes. But I believe you'll learn more about dancing by performing, rather than listening to some teacher who didn't have what it takes to make it as a performer."

"That makes total sense," Arianna said.

Dawn rolled her eyes. "Let's say you're right. What happens if she gets injured? What happens when she's too old to dance professionally?"

"We take very good care of our company. Many go on to start companies of their own. Some continue with our company as choreographers. Think about this. You're young, strong, talented. Do you want to waste your best years in a classroom and deny your earning potential?"

"Mom, do you know how much money I could make, how much we could save without paying tuition? I could be earning money so we could pay..."

"Hush," her mother said. "Look, mister. I'm not buying what you're selling. And we're late for class." She wrapped an arm around her daughter's shoulders and led her to the studio.

"Mom, we should at least listen to what he has to offer," the girl said.

Vincent caught up to them as they were entering the studio. "Look, Ms. Foster. I'm sorry I caught you off guard here. I'd really like to sit down with you and your daughter and talk about this opportunity. Maybe I could take you both to lunch, or perhaps dinner? Or, if you prefer, I can come to your house for a visit. No pressure." He held out his business card again. "Please, check out our website and if you're interested, give me a call."

Dawn Foster reluctantly took the card. "We'll see." She turned her attention to Mama Rose, who was standing at her desk, a scowl on her face. "Mama Rose, are you alright?"

"I'm fine." She turned her attention to the teen. "Arianna, you're late for class. Hurry up and get changed."

"Yes ma'am," Arianna said, shooting a look between her mother and the older woman. "Talk to you later Mr. D'Ambrosio." She scurried off, leaving the three adults.

"Mr. D'Ambrosio met us outside," Dawn said.

"Did he now," Rose replied.

"Mama Rose and I go way back," Vincent said, his smile bright. "It's been a long time."

"Not long enough," Rose muttered. "What did he say to you?"

"He saw some videos of Arianna and he wanted to offer her a position in his dance company," Dawn answered, her brow furrowing.

"Yes, I think she has what it takes to make it to the big time," Vincent said, adding a wink.

Rose inhaled slow and deep before responding. "Dawn, the kids' dance uniforms came back from the cleaners. Would you mind heading back and pulling them out of the plastic and taking all the cleaner's tags off? You know we don't want them irritating the kids when it's time to perform."

Dawn eyed both Rose and Vincent. Whatever was going on between them, she wanted no part of it. "Sure, Mama Rose. I'll take care of it." She headed down the same hallway her daughter had gone.

"Mama Rose," Vincent said drawing it out. "You're looking as beautiful as ever."

"You need to leave," Rose said.

"Aw, come on, Rose. Is that any way to treat family?" He reached over to hug her, but Rose whipped out a pair of scissors pointed at his chest.

"You better back up, pretty boy. I'll gladly go to prison if it means I can rid the world of your sadistic and trifling ass."

"Now, Mama Rose, that's not very Christ-like, is it?"

"God will forgive me."

Stacy grabbed her mother's hand before she was able to thrust the scissors forward. "Mama, no." She held them as she faced her ex-husband. Drawing in a shaky breath, she said, "What are you doing here, Vincent?"

"Hello, *Anastasia*," he said, drawing out her name like a purring cat. "You're looking more lovely than the last time I saw you." His eyes roamed up and down her leotard-clad figure, sending a chill down her spine. "I'm sorry I missed you at the party the other night. I heard you were under the weather. I do hope you're feeling better."

Stacy willed her knees to hold steady and her stomach to settle. "I'll ask again: What. Are. You. Doing. Here."

"A little birdie told me all about you and your little school. I wanted to come see for myself and congratulate you."

"He's trying to talk Arianna Foster into joining his cabal," Rose spit out.

A fire raged in Stacy. "Let's get one thing straight, Vincent. You stay away from me, you stay away from CCA, and you stay away from my students. *All* my students. You may be able to sweet talk a naïve sixteen-year-old, but I know who and what you are. I'll never let it happen, you understand?"

Vincent took a step forward, his grin slipping into a sneer. "And just what exactly am I, *Anastasia*? And how do you propose to stop me from taking anyone I want?"

A hand clamped on his shoulder from behind. "I think you need to leave," Cooper said, moving between Vincent and the women.

"Ah, Cooper Banks, our gallant host," Vincent said. He took another leering look at Stacy, who shivered despite herself. "I can see what piqued your interest, but trust me, it's nothing special."

Stacy gasped as Cooper snatched Vincent by the lapels of his jacket.

"Don't do it, son," Rose said. "He's not worth it."

Wordlessly, Cooper shoved the other man back. Vincent smoothed down the lapels of his jacket and headed for the exit. "I'll see you soon, *Anastasia*."

Cooper waited until Vincent was out the door before turning to the women. "Are you alright?" His gaze shifted from Rose to Stacy.

"We're fine," Rose answered. "Thank you."

Stacy exhaled; her eyes were wet with unshed tears. "You should leave as well." She turned and fled down the hall to her office.

Cooper stood still, stunned by her words. Rose came over and took his hand. "Thank you, Cooper. You saved an old woman from going to jail." She gave him a rueful smile. "Now go. Fix this." She gave him a gentle push in the direction her daughter had gone.

THIRTY

Stacy wrapped her arms around her knees and huddled in a beanbag in the corner of her office. She did nothing to stop the tears but prayed that her stomach would keep its contents down. After all these years, she still couldn't believe the effect Vincent had on her.

Vincent. How did he find out where she was? Why was he even at CCA? The last time she'd seen him before the night of the party had been at the courthouse when she was finalizing her divorce. He spent the entire proceeding staring at his phone, as his lawyer spoke on his behalf. Once the judge issued the final decree, he turned and looked at her and blew her a kiss. It was all she could do not to run out of the courtroom. It had taken a long time to rebuild her life and career and she was proud of what she'd accomplished. There was much more she would be able to do, thanks in large part to Cooper Banks' generosity.

Cooper. He'd declared his love for her, but then he'd turned around an invited Vincent back into her life. That kind of betrayal was unforgiveable. Why had she told him she loved him?

Because you do love him.

She shook her head. She thought she knew what love was. She had thought that with Vincent. She learned the hard way that Vincent was incapable of loving anyone other than himself. But Cooper had shown her real love. Not only was he generous with his money, but with his time, and with his spirit. He went out of his way to make sure that Stacy and those she cared about felt special. He wanted her to experience the kind of success she'd worked so hard for herself, her students, and her community. More importantly, he had made her feel safe and secure, something she never realized she needed.

Her head popped up at the soft knock on her door.

"Stacy?"

She groaned. "Please go, Cooper."

"Sweetheart, please let me in," he pleaded. "I just want to make sure you're okay. Please open the door."

She knew if she didn't let him in, he'd be waiting for her when she ended her day. Sighing, she went to the door and opened it. "I'm fine, see?"

"You're a terrible liar," he said, wiping a tear from her cheek.

For a second, she reveled in his caress, but then snatched her face away. Wiping her own tears, she pushed her shoulders back and stood up straighter. "I said I'm fine. What are you doing here anyway?"

"I came because you refused all my calls and didn't respond to any of my texts."

"I've been busy."

He arched an eyebrow and shook his head. "I just need five minutes to explain what happened. If you hear me out and still decide you don't want to be with me, I'll go. Just five minutes, please. I think what we have is worth that, don't you?"

He waited for a few agonizing seconds before she pulled the door back and gestured for him to take a seat. The cramped office contained a desk and computer chair, along with a couple of beanbags and a small love seat. In the back of his mind, Cooper decided that he was going to ensure Stacy had a much larger, more comfortable office in the new facility. *No more making decisions for her. I'll let her decide what she wants.* He took a seat on the loveseat while she resumed her place on the beanbag in the corner.

She checked the timer on her watch. "You have five minutes."

He nodded. "First of all, are you alright?"

"I told you, I'm fine. Four minutes, thirty seconds."

"In the few times we've talked about your ex, you never mentioned his name. Not once. I even tried to find out through public records, but apparently your marriage license and divorce decree have been sealed."

"The lawyers handled that. Three minutes, thirty seconds."

He let out a slow breath. "I had Felicity send out the invites. She created the guest list and set everything up. I never met Vincent until that night. I had no idea who he was. In fact, he wasn't even on the original guest list. He was a plus one for another guest, Cynthia Jackson, who is a generous arts patron. Apparently, she is in business with Vincent, and she thought it would be a good idea for the two of you to meet."

She snorted. "A little late for that."

"She either doesn't know his history with you or she didn't make the connection between your former life and your current one. When Felicity and Eric told me what happened to you and that Vincent was your ex, I was ready to throw him out on his ass."

"But you didn't."

He shook his head. "I couldn't. There were members of the media arriving, and the last thing I wanted was to give him any oxygen in the press by me kicking him out of the party. I made sure the story was about CCA, not him."

"Time's up." She stood up and went to open the door. "Thanks for coming and I appreciate what you did out there, but you should go."

He stood and walked to the door but stopped to face her. "So that's it?"

"You said you wanted to explain," she said, "and you did. I appreciate the explanation."

"Stacy…"

"What do you want from me, Cooper?" She flung out her hands. "You want forgiveness? Fine, you're forgiven. You want me to thank you? I already did."

"What I want is for you to understand that I never set out to hurt you. I love you, Stacy. And before the other night, you said you loved me."

She turned her head. "That was a mistake," she said.

"I don't believe it." He moved closer and took her hand. When she didn't remove it, he continued. "Stacy, you're my heart. You're my world. The thought of anyone hurting you guts me to the core." He took another step closer. "I am so sorry he caused you so much pain. And I'm so sorry that I was the one that brought that pain back into your life, even if it was unintentional." He reached over and turned her face so he could see it. The hurt that still registered in her eyes made him sick to his stomach. "I love you, Stacy. If you can look me in the eyes and tell me you don't love me, I'll leave and I'll never bother you again."

She swallowed past the lump in her throat, as the tears fell again. Her chin trembled, and she gripped his hand. "I…I love you, Cooper."

He pulled her into his arms and held her, kissing the top of her head, then pulling her face to his. As their lips met, a fire raged throughout his body, causing him to crush himself to her. She responded to the kiss, with him devouring her with his tongue, willing her to know the passion he felt inside.

The sound of footsteps in the hall penetrated their brains and they pulled back, clutching each other as they caught their breaths. He held her close, unwilling to break the connection flowing between them.

"Ahem." They turned to see Dawn Foster standing there with a huge grin on her face. "I'm sorry to interrupt."

"It's okay," Cooper said. "I was just about to leave."

"Stay," Stacy said, "please." She turned from his embrace but stayed close enough to feel his body heat. "What can I do for you, Dawn?"

"Mama Rose asked me to put the dance uniforms away," Dawn said. "I think she wanted me out of the room to deal with that Vincent dude."

Stacy stiffened. "Vincent D'Ambrosio? You met him? What did he want?"

Dawn nodded. "He came up to us as we were coming in. He said he worked with you, and he thought Arianna would be perfect to lead his company."

"What did you tell him?" Stacy asked.

"Nothing. Arianna practically jumped at the chance, but something about him rubbed me the wrong way. I wanted to get your thoughts on him and his offer."

Stacy felt Cooper's hands on her shoulders, and she silently thanked God for the strength he provided. "You are right to be skeptical. Let's just say Vincent makes a lot of promises that he can't keep. You'd be wise to steer clear of him."

"That's all I needed to hear," Dawn said. "Carry on," she added with a wink before departing.

Cooper could feel the tremors coursing through Stacy's body. He wrapped his arms around her. "I know what you're thinking."

She shook her head. "It's bad enough that he even set foot in my school, but to know he's trying to poach one of my students? My God, Cooper, if he put his hands on Ariana, I would kill him myself."

"I'll make sure you have plenty of money on your books." The chuckle she made relieved him. "I think it's time you told your story."

Stacy shook her head. "I said enough. Dawn is smart. She'll protect Arianna." She turned and wrapped herself in another embrace.

THIRTY-ONE

Cooper offered to cook dinner at Mama Rose's house. They invited Toye and Eric to join them. Stacy explained to Toye about the mix-up at the party and begged her friend to forgive Cooper. Toye reluctantly agreed to come to dinner, especially when she found out Eric was joining them.

"I really hope your girl will give my guy a break," Cooper said, adding the pasta to the pot of boiling water. "She really ripped him a new one when he called her later."

Stacy laughed. "I think it'll be fine. When I called to invite her to dinner, I explained what happened. She felt bad taking it out on Eric, but she was in defense mode. She's been my best friend and she was there through the whole Vincent mess. If it hadn't been for her and Mama, I don't know how I would have survived." She blinked back new tears as Cooper wrapped her in a hug.

"You didn't just survive," Mama Rose said, entering the kitchen, "you thrived. What that ugly devil meant for evil, God designed for your good. And not just for you, baby, but for all those children and their families whose lives you have changed."

"Thank you, Mama," Stacy whispered. Cooper planted a kiss on the older woman's forehead, then went back to his sauce.

"Remind me to apologize to Toye and thank her for being such a good friend to you," Cooper said.

"I think that new car you bought has earned you enough good will," Stacy said, grinning.

"Knock, knock," Toye called out, entering the front door. "Look what I found hanging out in the street." She pulled Eric in the door.

"They'll let anybody walk the streets these days," Cooper called out. He walked over and greeted Toye and gave his best friend some dap. "Glad you made it, bro."

"It was a good day today," Eric replied.

Stacy hugged her best friend. "I take it you two kissed and made up," she whispered into Toye's ear. Seeing her friend blush, she laughed. "Oh my god!"

"Ssshhh…" Toye said, grinning. "Why do you think we were late?"

❧ ☙

After dinner, the group moved to the living room, settling in for some lively conversation. Stacy and Cooper were loading up the dishwasher when her phone rang. "It's Dawn Foster," she said. "Hi Dawn… wait, slow down. What happened?" She listened on the other end, her expression growing cloudier by the second. She gripped the edge of the counter as Cooper steadied her. "Okay, yeah. I'll be right there."

"What happened," Cooper asked. Rose, Toye, and Eric joined them in the kitchen.

"Apparently, Vincent and Arianna have been texting since class. She's threatening to run away if her mother won't let her sign with Vincent."

"What?"

She shook her head. "I have to go talk to them. I don't know what to say."

"Yes, you do," Rose said. "You have to tell them the truth about that man."

"I don't think I can," Stacy whispered.

"You can," Toye added. "You're the strongest woman I know. Remember Philippians 4:13."

Stacy nodded. "For I can do everything through Christ, who gives me strength," she quoted. Cooper gave her a reassuring hug and she nodded. "I'm going."

"I'll drive," Cooper said.

As the couple left, Eric said, "Do you mind filling me in on what's going on?"

"I'll explain," Rose said, "but first, let's pray."

□

THIRTY-TWO

An agitated Dawn Foster opened her door to greet the couple. "Thank you for coming over. I'm so sorry for disturbing you like this, but I didn't know who else to call. Why is a grown man texting my sixteen-year-old daughter?"

"You did the right thing," Stacy said. "There are things I should have told you about Vincent from the beginning, but I was… well, frankly, I was too afraid and ashamed to say anything."

"Please have a seat," Dawn said. "I'll go get Arianna."

The couple took a seat on the couch. There were photos of Arianna all around the room, some of her dancing, some with her mother. "She really loves her daughter," Cooper said.

"She really does," Stacy replied. Cooper rose as Dawn and Arianna emerged from the hallway.

"Hey, Ms. Stacy. Hey, Mr. Banks. I don't know why mom called you," the sullen teen spouted. "I already told her what's up."

"You watch your mouth, young lady," Dawn said. "Don't act like you don't have no sense around company. Sit your tail down." She pointed a finger at a chair next to the couch. Arianna stomped over and flopped down into it.

"Arianna, your mother called me because she was concerned. I understand you just met Vincent today," Stacy said.

The girl rolled her eyes and sighed. "In person, yes."

"What does that mean," Dawn asked.

"He's been following me for a while on my socials. He DM'ed me and we've been chatting about me working with him."

"For how long?"

"It's no big deal, Mom!"

"I thought it was strange him showing up out of the blue like that at CCA," Dawn said. "And you standing there acting like you just met him. No wonder you're falling all over yourself trying to work with him."

"I checked him out, Mom. He's no rando perv. He's legit, and so is his offer. And if you don't let me sign, Vincent says I could petition to become an emancipated minor and I could go out on my own."

"Whoa," Cooper said, "Slow down a minute, Arianna. That's a drastic step, one reserved for extreme circumstances. You don't want to go down that road with your mother."

"What do you know about it? You don't know nothing about me and my mama."

"Watch your mouth, Ari," Dawn growled.

"I know she loves you," Cooper said. "I know she's concerned about your future, or she wouldn't have called Stacy."

"Why are you here anyway?" Arianna asked.

"Your mother asked me about Vincent," Stacy said. "I told her it wasn't a good idea for you to get involved with him. If you're serious about dance, he's not the kind of man that you want to put in charge of your career."

"He said you'd say that," the teen sneered. "He told me he used to work with you, that you weren't good enough to make the stage, and you quit because you weren't willing to sacrifice everything for it. Well, I am. I'm ready to give it my all and Vincent is going to help me get there."

"Is that what he said? That I wasn't good enough, that I wasn't willing to sacrifice?" She let out a long breath and swallowed beyond the hard lump in her throat. "May I have some water," she asked.

"Of course. Ari, go get a bottle of water," Dawn said.

Stacy turned to Cooper. "I don't know if I can do this."

He gripped her hand and gave it a squeeze. "You can. You have to. I'm right here with you."

Arianna returned and handed a bottle of water to Stacy. As she drank, Cooper pulled out his phone. He saw the smart TV mounted on the wall. "I want you to see something," he said. "May I connect to your TV?"

"Of course," Dawn replied. She grabbed the remote and turned it on.

He pulled up a video and projected it on the large screen. The YouTube video was the one he'd first seen of Stacy dancing under her real name. The mother and daughter were mesmerized.

"Is that you?" Arianna asked

Stacy nodded. "That was me almost twenty years ago."

"But why does the video say Anastasia?"

"Because that's my birth name, before I changed it. Before Vincent came into my life," Stacy said. She turned to the bewildered teen. "I was sixteen when I first met Vincent. He came around, supposedly looking for the next great dancer. He promised me the world and I was desperate to believe him. My home life, well, it wasn't good, and I wanted a way out. I fell in love with him, or so I thought. When I turned eighteen, I married him."

The gasps from both mother and daughter weren't surprising. Cooper pulled up another item on his phone, which projected on the screen. "When I was first thinking of investing in CCA, I did some research on Stacy. I found this article in Dance Magazine. She was named their most promising dancer that year."

"That's how Vincent found me," Stacy said. She took another sip of water. "He wanted me not just for his company, but for himself. When I married him, he took control of everything: my money, my appearance, my career. I did everything he asked of me and more. I wanted to please him not only as his wife, but as a performer. He took advantage of my desperation. He pushed me beyond my limits, and when I injured myself, he left me."

"Just like that?" Arianna asked.

"Yeah, just like that."

"Bastard," Dawn muttered.

"I thank God for my mother and my best friend. They helped me rebuild my life, and by the grace of God, I was able to start over and build CCA," Stacy concluded.

Arianna collapsed back in her seat. "How come you never told us this before? I've always wondered why you never danced professionally."

"I saw you on the stage with Alvin Ailey's group," Dawn added. "You belonged up there."

Stacy shrugged. "Part of it was shame, but mostly fear. I feared Vincent for so long, afraid of what he might do if he ever found me again. But when he showed up at the studio, I knew I couldn't let him get his hooks into you." She reached over and took the girl's hand. "Arianna, I know how much you love dance, and I believe you have a bright future ahead of you if you decide to become a professional. There are so many better ways to do that, and I can help you get there. There's Julliard, American Ballet Theater, Alvin Ailey, just to name a few. Please sweetheart, don't rush into a mistake that can you cost you everything with someone who does not have your best interest at heart."

Arianna swiped at the tears on her cheeks. "I hear you, Ms. Stacy. I'm sorry he treated you so bad." She turned to her mother. "I'm sorry, Mom. I should have told you what was up."

"It's okay, baby," Dawn said, "but I need you block him on your socials. Now."

The teen pulled out her phone and tapped it a few times. "Done," she said, showing her phone to her mother for confirmation. Everyone stood and Arianna gave Stacy a hug. "Thank you for telling me the truth, Ms. Stacy." She turned to Cooper. "Mr. Banks, did you mean what you said about helping us if I get into Alvin Ailey?"

He nodded. "That's a promise." He reached into his pocket and pulled out a business card and handed it to her mother. "That goes for any program she gets into. If you need short-term or long-term housing, or if you need to switch jobs, you get in touch with me." He shook Dawn's hand; they said their goodbyes and he escorted Stacy out to his car.

He started the engine but didn't pull off right away. Taking her hand, he brought it to his mouth and kissed it. "I'm so proud of you, sweetheart. I know that wasn't easy for you."

She nodded. "It had to be done." She thought for a moment. "Cooper?"

"Yeah?"

"Vincent has to be stopped. I think it's time I told my story. My whole story. Do you know someone who could help?"

He grinned. "I thought you'd never ask."

THIRTY-THREE

"Nervous? You're not planning to jump, are you?"

Stacy nudged Cooper. She turned her attention to the stunning lakefront view from Cooper's condo. "I'm nervous, but I'm too scared of heights to jump." She checked her watch. "She's late."

"I know. She just texted me. There was an accident on Lake Shore Drive. Traffic is backed up. She should be here shortly." Cooper led her away from the windows to the couch opposite of where her mother and Toye sat. "You want something to eat or drink?"

Stacy shook her head. "Just water for me."

"I'd like some tea, Cooper," Rose said. Toye declined anything and Cooper went to get their drinks.

"Tell the truth as you remember it," Toye said. "Don't embellish with what you presume his motives were. He can only refute your recollections, but we have the receipts." She opened her briefcase and pulled out a file folder and her iPad. "I have your hospital records and your depositions from the pre-trial conversations prior to the divorce."

"I thought the records were sealed," Rose said.

"The divorce proceedings are sealed. These were negotiations that we had at her lawyer's office. They were never entered into the divorce decree."

Cooper came back and gave the drinks to everyone. "She just texted. She should be up in about five minutes."

Rose stood. "Let's pray." Everyone stood and grabbed hands as Rose prayed. "Father, thank You for Your goodness and mercy. Father, Your word says that all things work together for the good of those who love you and are called according to your purpose. We are here because You have called us to this point in time. You have brought us to this place and time so that the truth could be revealed. I pray for my daughter, that she will put her faith and trust in You. I pray You will give her the courage to speak the truth, so that evil will be rebuked and revealed. I pray for the reporter that's coming that she will write the words which will allow the world to know the truth. Grant us this in Your son's mighty and matchless name, amen."

The doorbell rang. Cooper went to answer it, then led a petite redhead and a taller dark-haired man, who had a camera bag with him. Cooper made the introductions. "Miranda White, I'd like you to meet Stacy Roberts, her mother, Rose Roberts, and their friend and attorney, Toye Hawkins. Stacy, Rose, Toye, this is Miranda White. Miranda is a freelance writer whose work has been featured in Dance Magazine, as well as many national newspapers."

"It's a pleasure to meet you, Ms. White," Stacy said.

"The pleasure is mine, and please, call me Miranda. Full disclosure, I've done some write ups on Cooper and his foundation," the woman said. "We've gotten to know each other over the years, so I'm glad he asked me to write this story." She pointed to the bespectacled man who was setting up lights. "That's my photographer, Russell Stafford. He's going to take a few candid photos and then at the end we'll take more formal poses, if that's okay with you."

Stacy looked to Toye and her mother, who gave their assent. "That's fine."

"Why don't we take a seat," Cooper said. "Can I get either of you something to drink?"

"I'm fine," Miranda responded. Russell waved them off as he continued setting up his equipment. Once everyone was settled, Miranda pulled out her phone and her iPad and pencil. "I'd like to record this interview as well as take notes. It helps me get my facts straight. If at any time you want to speak off the record, please say so and I'll pause the recording. Does that work for everyone?"

"That's fine," Stacy said.

"Excellent. Let's get started. Tell me a little about yourself. How did you get into dancing in the first place."

Stacy relaxed a bit and began sharing her story. She told how her mother got her into dancing to channel her energy as a child. Rose added how she wanted to put something positive in her daughter's life and to keep her away from her verbally abusive stepfather. From an early age, Stacy's talent was evident, and she was on the fast track to a formal dance program and was weighing options when they met Vincent. They succumbed to his promises and charm, with Stacy eloping with him one week after her eighteenth birthday. Toye provided a copy of the marriage certificate.

As the conversation turned, Stacy began relaying details of her marriage, including the physical, emotional, and sexual abuse Vincent used against her. She detailed that she learned of his various affairs during her marriage from other members of the company. Finally, she shared the details of her injuries and how Vincent filed for divorce the day she learned she would never be able to perform professionally again. Toye provided all the documentation: photos of injuries, Stacy's medical records, the proof of service of the divorce. Toye also shared the terms of the negotiations for the divorce settlement, as well as Stacy's rationale for not pursuing support or filing charges against Vincent.

"I was under the false impression that no one would believe me," Stacy said. "Other than my mom, Toye, and my lawyer, no one would believe me if I said anything. Vincent told me that if I ever spoke out against him, I would be blackballed in the dance community. I guess he had been putting it out there that I was being a diva and difficult to work with. My injuries took care of that."

Miranda stopped writing and looked up. "This is damning information you've shared. You've waited over fifteen years to speak up. Why now?"

"Vincent found one of my young students online and began secretly communicating with her, trying to convince her he would make her a star in his company. When her mother learned what was happening, she reached out to me. I had to warn them about Vincent in order to protect them. It was with God's grace that I'd come through. I never wanted one of my most promising students to succumb to Vincent's twisted influence. If you'd like to speak with them, they are more than willing to share their version of the story."

"Your story is compelling to say the least," Miranda said. "I appreciate you taking the time to share it. But you have to know, despite all the evidence you've shared, some may perceive you as a woman scorned, a jealous ex. Or perhaps you're angry because he's trying to poach one of your students, who just may be your golden ticket back to the big leagues."

Stacy smiled. "I am not now, nor have I ever been, jealous of anything or anyone Vincent has. My primary concerns are building CCA and protecting my students from predators within this industry. It's hard enough to carve out a career in the arts, especially in dance, and especially for those of us of color. The last thing anyone needs is to be taken advantage of a by a predator masquerading as the gatekeeper for your career."

Miranda paused her recording. "I need to share something else with you. Ever since Cooper brought this story to my attention, I've been doing some digging. I've spoken with current and former members of his companies. The affairs are an open secret. But several women have detailed other allegations of abuse, including sexual assault. They kept silent because they were afraid of retribution not just from Vincent, but from the entire dance community. They were reluctant to go on the record. Once I share with them your story, I'm positive I will get more corroboration on the record."

"Tell me something," Stacy asked. "What made you take this story on?"

Miranda smiled. "I love to dance. I'm not very good at it, but I love it. I took lessons for years, but I always knew I'd never make a living at it. So, I did the next best thing: I began writing about it. I started covering the arts in college and that turned into my career. I've written many stories over the years, both good and bad, about the arts and those who support them. I've heard stories for years about abuses by directors, choreographers, even other dancers. It's only recently that artists are starting open up. The MeToo movement did wonders for actors, but the dance community has still been afraid to shed light in the darkness. Stories like yours and countless others will finally break the stigma of speaking up and calling out these abusers."

"Reporters like you are going to help end this cycle of abuse," Rose said.

"From your mouth," Miranda said. "Let's get some photos in and we're done for now."

"What happens next?" Stacy asked.

"I go back to my contacts, try and get them on the record. I'll finish up my story. Then I go to Vincent and get his side of the story. Of course, he's going to refute everything. I'm sure he'll have his PR team and lawyer on standby. I've already connected with some editors to run the article when I'm done. If all goes well, the story should be out in about a month. I'll send you a copy of the final story before it goes to press."

Once the photos were wrapped up and Miranda and Russell departed, Stacy leaned back on the couch and exhaled. "I think I could go for that drink now."

"I am so proud of you, sweetheart," Cooper said, wrapping an arm around her shoulders. He kissed her on the forehead. "I have a better idea. Why don't we go out and celebrate? I have it on good authority that Twila Dee is doing a pop-up concert tonight to preview her new album."

"Sounds like a plan to me," Rose said.

"You know I'm in," Toye added.

Stacy peered at her mother and best friend. "Ya'll never want to go out on a Thursday night.

"You know I love Twila," Rose said.

"I'm down for a good time any time," Toye said.

"I'm sure those tickets are sold out," Stacy said.

"I already got the tickets," Cooper said, with a grin.

"And what if I said no?"

"Then five people would have gotten very lucky tonight."

THIRTY-FOUR

The line to enter Winter's Jazz Club was out the door. When they pulled up, Stacy said, "We're never getting in. And if we do, we're going to be sitting in a corner."

"I got this," Cooper said. "Don't worry."

The limo driver pulled up to the sidewalk where a smiling Eric stood waiting. He gave hugs to everyone.

"How did you get here?" Toye asked.

"I came from work. The hospital is so close, it was easier to walk." He extended his arms to Toye and Rose. "Let's get inside. The show starts in a few minutes."

Cooper linked arms with Stacy and led the group. He presented the tickets and went inside.

The club was intimate, and the atmosphere was electric. The hostess led them to the front of the stage, where a couple of tables were open with a "Reserved" sign on them. "Nicely done, Cooper. How did you manage this," Stacy asked.

"I know people," he said, winking. They ordered drinks and small plates. By the time the drinks arrived, the audience was cheering for Twila Dee's entrance. She began her set, starting with her most popular Grammy-winning hit. After a couple of numbers, she took a moment to greet the audience.

"Hello Chicago! It's good to be home again!" She let the cheers go for a few minutes before continuing. "I'm so excited to be back in my hometown. This has been a whirlwind year for me. But none of it would have been possible without the help of one of my favorite people in the world, who just happens to be in the audience tonight. Please give a round of applause to the executive director of Chi City Arts, and the woman who gave me my foundation, Stacy Roberts! Take a bow, Ms. Stacy."

Stacy stood and waved briefly, then blew a kiss to her former student. As she took her seat, Twila continued. "I also see Stacy's mom, Mama Rose. Wow, Mama Rose, I never would have thought I'd see you at one of my concerts." She giggled along with the audience.

"One of the reasons I did this pop-up concert was because I wanted my fans here to get the news first. My second album is coming out soon!" The audience cheered. "Thank you! Tonight, I'm going to debut some new music from the album. But before I do, I'm excited because one of the songs I'm going to do is a remake of one of my favorite songs by one of Ms. Stacy's favorite artists, Lionel Richie."

The piano player began playing the first notes of a song. "The best part of this new recording is that it's going to be a duet with the one, the only, ladies and gentlemen, please welcome to the stage Mr. Lionel Richie!"

The audience jumped to their feet as the Grammy and Oscar-winning singer/songwriter/producer took the stage. He gave a hug to Twyla and waved to the audience. He took his place behind the keyboard and adjusted the microphone. He began playing the first notes to "Truly," as the audience applauded.

Lionel sang the first verse as smoothly as the first time he recorded it. As he came to end of the first verse, Cooper stood and held out his hand. "Dance with me."

"What are you doing?" Stacy said. "Sit down. This is the performance of a lifetime."

"I know," he said. "Dance with me."

Stacy glanced around. The music had stopped, and she blushed from embarrassment. The entire club was watching them.

"Dance with me," he repeated.

"Go on," Rose said.

"You're holding up the show," Toye whispered, giggling.

Sighing, Stacy placed her hand in Cooper's and stood. He pulled her into his arms and the music began again. They danced slowly, with Stacy looking around at the crowd. "I don't believe you did this. You know people are filming this."

"I don't care," Cooper said. "I only have eyes for you."

They continued their dance as Twila picked up the second verse of the song. Lionel and Twila joined in on the chorus. Stacy closed her eyes, relishing this moment. *Thank you, Father. I'm here with the man that I love, the man that You blessed me with. We're all healthy and happy, and finally at peace. This night could not get any better.*

The song ended and the audience cheered raucously. Stacy opened her eyes, only to see Cooper kneeling in front of her. "What are you doing?"

"I don't have any words better than the ones Lionel and Twila just sung. I am truly in love with you, Stacy Roberts. And with the blessing of your mother and best friend, and in front of all these strangers…," he reached into his pocket and pulled out princess cut diamond ring, surrounded by alternating amethysts and diamonds and slid it on her finger, "will you marry me?"

"Yes. Yes. Yes!" She leaned down and kissed him to the applause of the audience. They were joined by Rose, Toye, and Eric, who exchanged hugs with the happy couple. Twila came off the stage and gave them a hug. Lionel brought them to the stage to offer his congratulations and best wishes. A series of photos happened, then he bid farewell to the audience.

Twila resumed the show, brushing back her tears of joy for her former mentor. "Hey Chicago, I'm ready to sing!" The band struck up another song.

Stacy was blown away. A thousand questions were running through her head, and she knew she'd ask them in the limo on the way home. But one question she couldn't hold in. "How did you get Lionel Richie here?" Before Cooper could answer, she started laughing. "I know—you know people."

THIRTY-FIVE

It was a picture-perfect Saturday afternoon for Stacy and Cooper's engagement party. Wanting to include all of CCA, as well as family and friends, Cooper rented the South Shore Country Club. In addition to the live music and dancing, the couple wanted the children to have fun. They had several bouncy houses, face painters, balloon artists, and assorted games to keep the kids occupied. Stacy paid teens from her church to keep an eye on the children outside, while the adults enjoyed the party on the inside. The glass patio doors allowed the parents to keep an eye on the kids or to step outside in the sunshine.

Eric made the first toast. "I've known Cooper since our freshman year at Morehouse. He was a bit of a nerd. I took pity on him, taught him a few things, helped him get some game, of which he had none." Laughter erupted around the room. "What I did not have to help him with were the things that made him the man he is: kind, generous, smart. When he met Stacy, he met a woman with those exact same qualities—and she was gorgeous to boot." More laughter. "I watched them become friends, fall in love, and I'm happy that my best friend has found the love of his life. Raise your glass to Cooper and Stacy!"

"Cooper and Stacy," the guests replied.

Midway through dinner, Toye stood. "Stacy and Cooper. My best friend has been through a lot in life, and she's come out stronger and better than ever. I warned Cooper that if he hurt her, I would hurt him. He hasn't yet, so I guess I'll agree to the marriage." She allowed for more laughter. "Stacy and Cooper, may your latter days be the best days of your life. I love you both. Cheers."

Following dinner, the band began playing "Silly." Cooper and Stacy took to the dance floor once again, engaging in the waltz she had taught him. She couldn't stop smiling at his serious nature and she could tell he was counting in his head. "You're doing fine," she whispered.

"Easy for you to say," he whispered back. The song ended and the crowd applauded. They took a bow and Cooper wiped his forehead. "I don't remember that being so exhausting."

"You thought that was bad? I have a surprise." She turned to the DJ. "Hey DJ, drop that beat!"

The DJ put on the "Cha Cha Slide," bringing everyone to the floor. The crowd enjoyed the dance and kept going as the "Cupid Shuffle" then "The Wobble" were played. After twenty minutes of dancing, Stacy and Cooper took to their seats. They downed a couple of glasses of water, then continued greeting their guests.

Cooper was catching up with some Morehouse alums, so Stacy took the moment to slip away. "I'm heading to the restroom," she told Toye.

"Check your makeup. We have pictures in ten minutes."

❧ ☙

Stacy took a final look in the mirror. Her makeup was camera ready, her hair smoothed back into a sleek ponytail. She glanced at her engagement ring. It was sheer perfection, down to the cut and colors. She was sure her mother and Toye had helped Cooper design it.

She took a spin in her dress. The lavender sundress was flowy and light and was perfect for dancing. Cooper had opted for a tan suit with a lavender shirt. The photos were scheduled to be taken on the lawn. She checked her watch and knew she had only minutes to get to the spot they had picked out near the lake. She went to the door, yanked it open, then stumbled back.

"Hello, Anastasia."

"Vincent," she breathed.

Cooper checked his watch. "How long does it take to check your makeup?"

"Are you kidding?" Toye said. "It takes effort to look effortlessly beautiful."

"I'm sure," Cooper said. "I'm going to go get her."

"You need to leave," Stacy said.

"I don't think so," Vincent replied. "You and I have unfinished business."

"Our business was finished a long time ago."

She tried to leave, but Vincent slammed his hand against the door jamb, blocking her path. "You'll leave when I say you can leave. Or have you forgotten what I taught you, Anastasia?"

She looked up at her ex. Underneath his bloodshot eyes, bags had formed and began bulging. There were more wrinkles around his face. His normally close-cropped hair had grown out into an uneven afro. His crisp beard had grown out in scraggly wisps. He looked less like a professor and more like an old, worn-out man. Whatever it was about his physical stature that frightened her was gone. "My name is Stacy. And I don't have to do anything you say ever again."

"Like hell," he growled. He pulled a newspaper article out of his pocket. "You did this! And you're going to pay."

❧ ☙

Cooper was working his way through the crowd, shaking hands, and accepting congratulations. Rose came up to him. "Is everything alright, Cooper?"

"It's nothing, Mama Rose. I'm just looking for my bride-to-be. She's supposed to be with me taking our engagement photos."

A worried look crossed the older woman's face. "I'm coming with you."

❧ ☙

"I stand by what I said. I told the truth. And apparently, I wasn't the only one that had something to say," Stacy said.

"You're a lying bitch! You destroyed me! Dancers quit, my partners pulled out, our shows have been cancelled. All because you couldn't keep your mouth shut." He grabbed her left hand. "Well, I see you snatched up another money man.

When I'm done with you, he'll toss you aside like the trash that you are."

Stacy opened her mouth to scream, but before she could, Cooper grabbed Vincent's shoulder, spun him around and punched him in the gut. Vincent doubled over. He straightened up and tried to take a swing at Cooper, but he grabbed Vincent by the lapels of his suit jacket.

"I am by nature not a violent man. But I swear before God, if you come after my family ever again, I will destroy you. If you even think about trying to start up another dance troupe, company, whatever, I will bankrupt it before it even gets started. I will make it known to anyone that thinks of hiring you that I will buy them out and fire you. You are done terrorizing women, you understand!"

Rose and Toye came up behind them, followed by Eric and several Morehouse alums. "Is there a problem," Eric asked.

"No, there's no problem here," Cooper said. He slammed Vincent against a wall, then drew Stacy to his side. "Please escort this gentleman off the premises."

"We got you, bro," one of the men said. He and another man grabbed Vincent and began half-dragging him out of the facility.

"Are you alright?" Rose asked her daughter.

"I'm fine," Stacy said. "I'm just fine." She looked up at Cooper. "Aren't we late for pictures?"

He leaned in and gave his fiancée a kiss. "Yes ma'am. Let's go."

THIRTY-SIX

Eighteen months later…

"Stacy! Honey, we need to get going," Cooper called out. "The car is here. We don't want to be late."

His wife came out of their bedroom, adjusting an earring. "I'm coming. I just needed to change my outfit which means I had to change my jewelry." She stopped and stared at him. "What? Do I look alright?"

Love and desire shared equal space on Cooper's face and in his heart. "You look amazing. But why did you change? The dress was gorgeous."

"It didn't fit right. Besides, it's a groundbreaking ceremony and I didn't think I should show up in a mini dress. This pantsuit is more comfortable." She did a quick twirl. The three layers of the bodice fluttered in the breeze then settled over her figure.

"Baby, you could show up naked and be stunning."

"Wouldn't that go viral. I can see the headline now: 'Billionaire wife and youth director shows up naked at groundbreaking.' The mayor and the governor would be so pleased." They laughed and headed for the door.

Downstairs in the car, Mama Rose was waiting for them. "I was beginning to think I was going to have come up and get you," she scolded as the couple slid into their seats. "We can't keep the mayor and the governor waiting."

"No, we cannot," Cooper said, winking at his mother-in-law.

"Sorry, Mama," Stacy said. "Had to make some adjustments."

Her mother patted her on the hand. "You feeling alright?"

"I'm doing just fine, Ma."

They chatted during the drive, excited for the day they had been anticipating for so long. Stacy marveled at how God had worked things out. Two years ago, she was fighting to keep the doors open. She was alone and weighed down by her past. But God had seen fit to send Cooper Banks into her life, not just to bring new life to CCA, but to show her the power of real love.

"Sweetheart, are you alright?" Cooper asked.

She nodded, swiping at a stray tear. "I was just marveling at God's goodness. I can't believe this day is finally happening."

"Oh hallelujah," Rose called out. "He's a prayer-answering God."

"Amen," Cooper said.

The car came to a stop, and they climbed out. The photographer, Russell Stafford, was waiting to take photos as they made their way to the podium. Most of the CCA students, parents and staff were present cheering them on.

Arianna and Dawn Foster came over to greet them. "We made it," Arianna said, "thanks to Cooper."

"I'm so happy you're here!" Stacy said. "How did the summer intensive go?"

"Terrific," Arianna said. "I'll be more than ready to start at Fordham next year."

"I am so proud of you," Stacy said, giving the young woman a hug. "And how are you, Dawn?"

"I'm doing great," the woman said. "I love my job at the MBIY Foundation, thank you, boss," she said, grinning at Cooper. "With the scholarships she's earning, I'll only have to pay for her housing and miscellaneous costs."

"And I've already met my future roommates," Arianna said. "We've been making plans since the summer."

"That's wonderful," Stacy said.

Cooper tugged at her arm. "We need to be going. We'll catch up after." They made their way to the podium and began greeting the mayor and the governor and assorted dignitaries and board members. They took their seats, and the ceremony began. Following remarks from the assorted politicians, Cooper and Stacy took turns thanking everyone for coming and making the day possible.

Finally, they descended off the platform and made their way to the area for the groundbreaking. Felicity coordinated handing out the hard hats and shovels to everyone and they posed for the requisite pictures. Russell was there capturing every moment.

Miranda came up and shook hands with the couple. "I love writing these kinds of stories," she said. "This is what the arts should be about."

"I can't thank you enough for your reporting on Vincent," Stacy said. "I didn't realize how freeing it would be to tell my story."

"I should be thanking you," Miranda said. "Not only did your story help break the silence, but I'm up for a Pulitzer."

"Congratulations," Cooper said. "Well done."

"There's still more," Miranda said. "A source told me that Vincent is pleading guilty to several charges including harassment and intimidation. Apparently, his lawyer advised that the only way he'll see the outside of a cell in the last half of his life is if he took a deal for fifteen years, twelve with good time. It's not nearly long enough, but at least he'll be held accountable for some of what he's done. He'll be an old man when he gets out."

"At least he won't be able to terrorize any more women," Stacy said.

"Amen," Cooper added.

"So, what's next for you," Miranda asked. "You've got the new CCA building coming. Any other news to share?"

"Well," Cooper said. He looked at his wife, who nodded her agreement. He wrapped his arms around her growing abdomen and said, "We're also pretty focused on our newest project under construction, coming in about five months."

AUTHOR NOTES

Thank you so much for reading! I hope you enjoyed Stacy and Cooper's story. I had so much fun writing it!

When I first started selling my books at author events, I'd offer up a CD of music referenced in or inspired by each story. Readers loved it! But times have changed, and we are in the digital age. Instead of a CD, I've created a playlist on Spotify of music just for this story: https://spoti.fi/3DurtmF

ACKNOWLEDGMENTS

First, last, and always, I give thanks to my Heavenly Father for my life and for this gift of writing. The more I learn about Him as Creator and Artist, the more I understand that creative writing is an expression of love and worship. May it forever be so.

My husband and sons are everything. I am grateful for their love and support. You are my greatest blessings.

My sisters-in-writing and fellow divas, Daphine Robinson and Cherlisa Richardson: God knew what He was doing when He brought us together! Grateful to have you as my besties and writing partners.

Special thanks to the Kindle Vella Divas—LaShaunda, Sylvia, Suprina, Danyelle, Rovenia, Paulette, and Taisha, for all your support, advice, and fantastic tips on promotion and publishing!

Finally, thank you to my fans and readers! I'm grateful that you keep coming back for more, even if I'm especially slow. Without you, I'd be writing for myself. It's more fun to share stories with others. If you enjoyed this story, please post a review and tell a friend.

May peace and blessings be upon you.

Until next time!

ACKNOWLEDGMENTS

ADDITIONAL BOOKS

Romance

A Decent Proposal

Rescued for Love

Contemporary Fiction

Journey to Jordan

Joy's Gift

Coming Soon

More Than a Conqueror

(Read on for a sneak peek)

MORE THAN A CONQUEROR

Donna Deloney

ONE

Get up. Leave your desk. And don't look back. Go. Now.

The email was from one of her co-workers. She glanced around the office, trying to figure out if she was being punked. Yet, everywhere she looked, people were plugged in, isolated, chained to their desks by the tethers of their headphones.

She read the email again. And again.

Looking around, she tried to find the sender, but he was nowhere to be found. In fact, she didn't see him come in at all that day. He was usually one of the first ones in, always stopping by her desk to greet her good morning and catch up on the latest gossip. But he wasn't in—she was sure of it. Yet, he hadn't called to take the day off either.

Is this some kind of joke?

She saw a couple of people checking their emails. Had they received it, too? What were they doing? Were they—like her—thinking this was some sort of humorous elaborate scheme?

Another email popped up: *Final warning. Get out. NOW!!!*

Her heart beat faster, and sweat pooled under her breasts despite the chill of the air conditioning.

One of her co-workers came her way. "Let's go."

"You can't be serious."

"I am. Grab your purse, and let's get out of here. If it's a joke, we can say we just went for a walk."

"And if it's not?"

"Do you want to stick around to find out?"

The question sent chills down her spine. She grabbed her purse and shoved a couple of photos into the bag, trying not to draw attention to herself.

"Shouldn't we tell people? Should we call the police?"

"And say what? We got creepy emails based on an inside joke?"

"If it's true, and we leave them behind..."

"We'll figure it out later. Let's go!"

She stood and followed her friend out the side door. In the corridor, she saw him. And she knew. It was no joke.

They had barely made it down one flight of stairs when the first shots rang out.

TWO

"Miss Thornton? Are you with me?"

Danae Thornton blinked. She tried to refocus her attention on the man sitting across the table from her. *What is he saying? Who is this? C'mon, Danae...think, girl!*

"I'm sorry." Her raucous voice was barely audible as her throat tightened up. "May I...may I have a glass of water?"

The man nodded, then excused himself.

Danae looked around the room. *I'm at the police station. The man is a detective. Oh, God. The shooting.*

When the detective reentered the room, he set a bottle of water on her side of the table and took the seat across from her. He waited until she took several gulps before asking, "Better?"

Danae nodded. "Yes, thank you, Detective…"

"Detective Fisher. Are you okay?"

"I am." She took another gulp from the bottle.

"Can you go on?"

"Go on?"

"You were giving me a statement about the shooting," he said gently.

"The shooting. Yes, that's right. I didn't actually witness the shooting."

"So you've said." He pulled out his notebook and looked over his notes. "You left the office before the shooting started."

"Yes."

"Why?"

"Why what?" Danae asked.

"Why did you leave the office when you did?"

"Willa said we had to."

"Willa Jones, your co-worker?"

"Yes."

"Why did Ms. Jones insist you both leave?"

"The email."

"Yes, the email. 'Get up. Leave your desk.' You were reluctant to leave, but Ms. Jones insisted that you do. Did she know what was about to happen?"

"I don't think so."

"Yet, you let her talk you into leaving right before your colleague, Joseph Kelly, walked into your office and shot thirteen people, killing seven and wounding six before committing suicide."

"That's right."

"Okay, talk me through the morning."

"Again?"

"Yes. Don't leave anything out, no matter how trivial."

Danae sighed. "We've been over this."

"And we'll keep going over this until I'm satisfied," Fisher growled, his blue-green eyes boring into her watery brown ones.

"Do I need a lawyer?" Danae squeaked.

He leaned back in his chair. "You're not under arrest, Miss Thornton. I'm asking for your cooperation. You have to understand that you and Ms. Jones were the only ones to walk away unscathed. We need answers. The families need answers. The media wants answers. And since Mr. Kelly is dead, you and Ms. Jones are our only hope."

"But that's my point. I don't have answers. I don't know why he did this."

"He sent the email to you. To warn you."

"Yes."

"Why you? Why, Ms. Jones?"

Danae shrugged. "It was a joke."

"A joke?" Fisher frowned. "Eight people are dead, and six are wounded—two of which are in very critical condition. And you're saying this was a joke?!"

"No, no...that's not what I meant."

"What did you mean?"

"It was...I mean, we had a joke. It was a running joke."

"What kind of joke?"

"We used to joke around—Joe, Willa, and me—you know, when we would get frustrated with our jobs. We would jokingly say: 'If you get the email, you better run.'"

"You joked about killing people at work?"

"We weren't serious! It's just something you say."

"Apparently, Mr. Kelly didn't get the joke."

Danae took another gulp. "I don't understand."

"What don't you understand?"

"Why he did this. We joked about stuff like this all the time. Haven't you ever had one of those days where you want to punch your boss or blow something up?"

Fisher chuckled, his salt and pepper mustache twitching. "Yeah, I suppose."

"But you'd never actually do it, right?"

"No."

"Neither would I. Neither would Willa. That's why I don't understand what set Joe off."

Detective Fisher leaned back into his seat. "So, you get up, get to work. Then what?"

"I..." She paused to think. "I put my stuff away, booted up my computer, then went to get a cup of coffee from the pantry."

"After you booted up the computer?"

"Yes. The computer takes a while to get going. By the time I get my coffee, it's usually ready to go."

"Did you talk to anyone?"

"I said hello to a few people. I met Willa in the pantry."

"And?"

"And what?"

"What did you talk about?"

She shrugged. "Nothing important. Our plans for the weekend… That sort of thing. Just small talk. Getting ready for the day."

"Did you talk about Joe?"

"Not really. Wait, I did say that I thought it was weird he wasn't there. He was usually at work by the time we arrived."

"So, it was odd that he was running late?"

"Yes. He was always at work unless sick or on vacation, and he wasn't scheduled for vacation. If he was sick, Willa would have told me. Or he would have texted me."

"Did he normally do that?"

"Text me?"

"Yes."

She shrugged again. "Sometimes. We were friends. Not bosom buddies or anything, but we'd sometimes text if something was happening, and we didn't want to communicate it through email."

"Such as?"

"Is this really necessary?"

"Please."

Danae took another drink of water. The bottle was nearly three-quarters empty.

"You know, if stuff happened—somebody got chewed out, cussed out. You don't put that in an email in case they are reading."

Detective Fisher nodded and jotted a few notes.

"So, you and Ms. Jones had not heard from Mr. Kelly, which you thought was odd. What did Ms. Jones think?"

"I think she assumed he was stuck in traffic. I guess she didn't think much of it either."

"I see. What happened next?"

"I grabbed my coffee and went back to my desk. The computer was on, so I opened up my email."

"And you saw the note from Mr. Kelly."

"Yes."

"What did you think when you saw it?"

"That I was being punked—that Joe decided to try and get a rise out of me. Until Willa came by, I didn't even know if Joe had sent it to anyone else." She shook her head. "I can't believe he actually did this. Why would he do this?"

"We're not sure at this time. Other detectives are searching his house, his personal computer, emails, any correspondence. Hopefully, he left a note or some clue somewhere. Honestly, since he killed himself, it's a moot point, but it helps bring some sense of closure for the victims and their families."

"I need to know, too."

Fisher nodded. "I'll let you know as soon as we come up with anything. Now, can you tell me what happened next?"

Danae shrugged again. "You pretty much know what happened. I hesitated at first when Willa came by, but then, I followed her. I grabbed my stuff, and we left. Then I saw Joe."

And I alone have escaped to tell you.

"Did you say anything to him? Or he to you?"

"No. I just fixated on his eyes. And then Willa dragged me to the stairs." She took another drink of water. "I should have done something... I wish I knew..." She looked up at the detective. "What should I have done? Should I have tried to stop him, reason with him? Should I have warned the others? What was I supposed to do? They don't give you those kinds of instructions during orientation. I mean, you see this stuff on the news, and you think, 'I would have done something,' but that means nothing when you're face to face with...with..."

She let the tears trickle down her face.

"With a friend," Fisher said softly, then reached over and slid a box of tissue in front of her. "I don't know what you could have done, Miss Thornton. My perspective as a police officer is different from that of a civilian. If you tried to confront him, for all I know, you could have ended up being his first victim." He closed his notebook. "It's been a long day. Why don't you go home and try and get some rest? If I have any more questions, I'll contact you."

"I don't… my car..."

"I'll have an officer take you to your car. Take care, Miss Thornton. I'll be in touch."

As he escorted her to the door, she paused. "May I ask you a question, Detective?"

"Of course."

"Have you seen anything like this?"

A mixture of sadness and weariness flashed across his face. With slumped shoulders, he answered, "Far too many times. I always hope it will be the last, and I'm disappointed every time."

More Than a Conqueror

Coming in 2024

Made in the USA
Monee, IL
25 July 2025

21473590R00125